# THE OLD MEN
# WHO ROW BOATS

*& Other Stories*

## DAVID JOSEPH

Published by Portal 6 Press
A number of stories in this collection have previously appeared elsewhere: "The Old Men Who Row Boats" in *The London Magazine*, "The Gin Club" in *The Poydras Review*, "The Bullring" in *Typishly*, "The Cliffs" in *The Raven's Perch*, "The Cleanest Alimentación in Spain" in *Sunspot Literary Magazine*, "The Jeweler's Hands" in *Twist and Twain*, and "Lino" in *The Hong Kong Review*.

Edited by Emma Moylan
Cover by Booklerk
ISBN: 978-1-7359191-1-9

*For my parents, who meant the world and left it far too
soon, and for my wife Karen, who picked up the pieces and
keeps them together to this day.*

# ACKNOWLEDGMENTS

When I first began this project, I wasn't even sure it was ever going to amount to a book. At the time, we were traveling in Portugal, and a single story was born out of what began as a long poem. I hadn't planned to write a story or planned to write on this trip at all. But there I was, with the fragments of a story racing through my head, writing.

My graduate school advisor, James Ragan, used to tell us that you "chase a poem until it catches you" and I think the same thing can be said for stories. However, in this case it was the other way around. The stories in this book "chased" me down over the course of four years. I did my best to do them justice and bring them to life. At times, the stories asked a lot of me. I can only say that I did all I could to answer the call when they arrived at my door.

There are so many people to thank regarding this project that it's difficult to know where to begin. But I think I have to start with Jim Crenner, the college professor who inspired me to take the risks to write in the first place. To this day, more than twenty-five years since I graduated from college, I am very fortunate to still have him as both a mentor and a friend. What an incredible gift.

I would also like to thank some people who helped me bring this project to its conclusion. To my editor, Emma Moylan, thank you so much for your time and effort to pour over these pages with diligence and care and great skill. It is my good fortune to be able to work with such a gifted editor, and I am incredibly grateful for your guidance and counsel at every turn. Next, they say you can't judge a book by its cover, but in this case, I hope you can. I want to thank Booklerk for their commitment to creating this beautiful cover that I sincerely hope reflects what the pages inside might have to offer.

Lastly, these acknowledgments would not be complete without mentioning my family. To my sons, Jackson and Cassius, thank you for your patience during this process, for giving me the time to disappear into these stories, and for all of your love and support. And finally, to my wife, Karen, who this book is dedicated to, thank you for being all things to me—wife, editor (more often than you've asked to be), the love of my life, and always … my best friend. You've suffered alongside me the most, and I hope the publication of this book is a small reward.

# TABLE OF CONTENTS

# THE OLD MEN WHO
# ROW BOATS

I n Madrid, not far from the great museums that line the streets, old men row boats in the morning hours at Retiro Park. These are old men, but these are small boats. There is no vast sea here, just a man-made body of water surrounded by tourists and a stone monument flooded with birds. With the morning light emerging, these men set out in rowboats, leaning back as far as their aging spines will allow. Across calm waters, the men maneuver the oars. They maneuver the oars with poise, letting them enter the surface almost silently, propelling the boats backward without words.

Here, they rent boats by the hour. There are no destinations, just patterned ripples in the water, with the sun rising gently and the early morning joggers circling like gulls. They are old men with the bodies of old men, and rowing offers them physical activity. It allows for their limbs to move the way they did years before, and it requires a measure of coordination and strength. It provides the men with just enough work to make them feel as if they are still men, with the virility of men, capable of doing manly things. Alone in a boat, with nothing but their thoughts, oars, perhaps a wind jacket on mornings when the gusts blow stronger, the old men don't need to rely on anyone else. They are out of the way of the joggers and strollers, and they move unimpeded to their own rhythms, their independence temporarily restored, with knees bent and legs stretched out before them. Javier was one of those men who rowed boats.

Javier lived in a small apartment near the Reina Sofía Museum. The Reina Sofía was a glorious monument to modern art, perched just across the way from the Atocha train station in the heart of Madrid. Although there was nothing modern about Javier, he liked to go to the museum, and he liked to go there very often. He liked to go there and ride the modern glass elevator up and walk down the sterile halls until he stood squarely in front of *Guernica*, Pablo Picasso's masterpiece.

Javier felt an unspoken bond with Picasso and with *Guernica*. They shared a lot of time together at the Reina Sofía, but it was more than that. They shared a history of compassion, of understanding. Picasso wasn't a soldier, but he knew war and he knew pain. *Guernica* captured the horrors of battle and destruction, and Javier liked to stand in front of the painting, letting the images wash over him, into him. Javier wasn't a painter, but he had been a soldier, and he knew what it was like to feel the despair that one can only feel in the presence of death, the presence of unnatural death. There was nothing glamorous or glorious about it, and soldiers weren't so much brave as dutiful in his opinion. He had done his duty and he had seen great loss. Standing in front of *Guernica* reminded him that Picasso had too, that he wasn't alone, and that even the greatest atrocities could be beautiful when depicted in art. They were hauntingly beautiful for the manner in which they conveyed a moment in time, and they summoned powerful feelings in those who gazed upon their canvases. *Guernica* was such a painting, and people young and old, from all over the world, came to the museum to see it.

One of the things Javier liked about the *Guernica* exhibit was that small replications of Picasso's drafts of the painting were lined up on the opposite wall. Here, Javier had the chance to see the sketches and analyze them. Javier thought it was fascinating to consider what Picasso had included in his early drawings, what he chose to omit, and what he decided to add later on. These alterations had fundamentally changed the complexion of the painting. They altered the narrative. Most people only see the finished product, he thought. Few ever obtain a real sense of what it took for the artist to arrive here, on the precipice of greatness. This was the case in nearly every profession. We love or despise the shell, the veneer, the facade, with very little knowledge of what sits beneath, the underbelly, where the substantive quality often lies.

Most people walked into the room at the Reina Sofía unaware of the drawings on the opposite wall. They walked in and were, understandably, overwhelmed by the massive canvas sweeping across the wall before their eyes. The size and scope of the piece are truly astounding, and it wasn't unusual to hear people gasp upon seeing it for the first time. The painting literally took their breath away. It was that magnificent, a remarkable tour de force of emotion and power and possibility, and Javier always enjoyed being in the same room as the great painting.

And yet, he often found himself standing with his back to the canvas and to the crowds, as he gazed upon the sequence of drawings that had brought *Guernica* to its eventual conclusion, its inevitable conclusion. He was curious about Picasso's thought process, his experiments with different images, and what ultimately brought him to this most terrifying conclusion that would be the finished piece. It seemed unfathomable that Picasso could draw in a manner that was both childlike and spare and still find ways to illuminate the absolute terror that people felt, innocent people, who found themselves in the wrong place at the wrong time. The painting captured an element of fate, but the drawings revealed that this piece was, although well-conceived, born from raw emotion, from reaction, and only later did it become a more appropriately detached response to the day the village was bombed. Javier was continually struck by the distance between the first sketch and the original, and he envied Picasso's ability to go back, remove things, and reshape the narrative. War didn't allow you to do that. It was final and unforgiving, and there were no second drafts or revisions.

Javier had been in the navy. He liked the water, and he enjoyed working on ships. Being on the water made him feel like the world was endless, adrift in the vast, blue sea, completely aware of his infinitesimal place in the universe. This was where Javier felt most comfortable. He didn't fear the sea, the way it could rear its head at any moment. He embraced it. Whenever he was caught in a storm, he felt an uncommon sense of calm. The boat wasn't likely to sink. You just needed to ride it out and move through the ups and downs. Sometimes, you were tossed clear across the deck, and other times you just rolled gently over modest undulations. Either way, you were a passenger of sorts. The only choice was to accept it, to lean in, and to find a way to let nature know you weren't ever going to fight her—come what may. Javier could make peace with the elements regardless of the consequences. The actions of men were harder to accept.

In the mornings, Javier would leave his small apartment and head for the park. He would stop briefly for a cup of coffee and a tostada with olive oil and fresh, blended tomato. He always stopped at the same place, and they knew his order. He sat calmly and drank his coffee. He liked to drink coffee before he headed for the boat. It warmed the insides of his body, and it reminded him of those days when he needed to be prepared for a brisk wind out on the open seas. The coffee was good, and the people who worked there were always agreeable. He sat near the window, looking out at the busy street and dreaming of the open seas while cars rushed by.

From there, Javier would walk past the elegant Palace Hotel, where many great dignitaries had stayed, and head past the Ritz and up toward Retiro Park. It was only a slight incline, but he felt it more than he had in his youth. The ground wasn't like the water, he thought. Although it didn't move, it provided an element of resistance that he felt in his spine, in the base joints of his knees, and he longed to get inside the boat. Inside the boat, things were easier. The world was less complicated, and even his body responded in a way that seemed to forget how old it was.

These rowboats were primarily rented by tourists, usually later in the day, perhaps with their children, when the sun was high in the sky and a warm glow eased over the water. Javier liked to arrive before the day took flight, and he was always the first man through the turnstile. He was the first man through the turnstile, and he was always alone. He had spent years on boats with men, many of whom were now dead. He had liked the camaraderie then, but now he liked to be alone in the boat. He was nearly always alone, and this was comfortable for him. He never married, and he had no children. He was alone, but he wasn't lonely. They weren't the same at all, he thought, and he liked to take to the water with only himself in the boat. There would be nobody else to take care of or instruct. There would be nobody who required he make idle conversation, and Javier could simply sit down in the boat, grab the oars, take a deep breath, and propel his small craft backward across the man-made body of water.

On his way home from the park, he would often eat lunch near the museum and stop in to see *Guernica* in the early afternoon. This was a nice time of day to see the painting, and Javier liked to go to the Reina Sofía when fewer tourists were there. He liked that it was near his apartment, and he liked that it was bright and clean. Most of all, Javier liked that Picasso's *Guernica* was there. It was an added benefit that he liked one of the docents.

She was slightly younger than Javier, in her early seventies, he estimated. She was tall and lean and had let her hair grow gray. Perhaps gray wasn't the best description. It was silver, after all, with a fresh sheen, and she wore it magnificently. The lines on her face magnified her age, but she carried herself with an elegance that was uncommon. It was uncommon, and her poise was unmistakable. This was only the case in women who had lived to the point where there was nothing left to prove. Javier had searched the world over for a woman like that, only to come up empty.

The docent had an air of nobility about her, but it was nobility void of ego and arrogance. She was old enough to have seen her beauty fade, but she was young enough to remember before it had. Still, she glided through the museum halls with a contentment, a knowingness of the past and acceptance of the present that seemed to allow her to age with unusual ease, to smile more willingly, and to say hello with an affection that illustrated how terribly unaffected she was by the passage of time. This quality was incredibly attractive to Javier, and he always looked forward to crossing paths with her on his stops to see *Guernica*. Javier tried to visit the museum multiple times a week.

In fact, Javier visited the museum so often that it almost seemed as if he was coming by to check on *Guernica*, to make sure it was still hanging on the wall, that it hadn't been touched or damaged or moved without his permission. The painting meant a great deal to him, and he felt a sort of ownership over the canvas. He counted on it, needed it, and so he felt compelled to look in on *Guernica* on a regular basis.

Now that Spain had moved beyond the era of Franco, *Guernica* served as an important reminder of the past for Javier. He watched the young people in Madrid, and he knew they couldn't really fathom the Spain of Franco and that the civil war was merely something they learned about in school. They lived with freedoms in the wake of the unimaginable horrors that befell the people of Guernica, who were bombed so savagely and cowardly by Hitler in 1937.

But, to Javier, *Guernica* wasn't simply a painting about war or even the Spanish Civil War or even Franco for that matter. It was a painting about the innocent. It was a painting about children who deserve to be safe and protected, about mothers who bring them into the world, and it reflected their vulnerability amidst the savageness of warfare, cold and soulless and without a moral code. It was about pain and fear and unexpected death and destruction. And it was about Spain—the bull and the horse forever linked, intertwined both in the bullring and outside of it, evoking pride and pain in the hearts of Spaniards the country over. Yes. This was his Guernica, his Spain, and stopping by the Reina Sofía made him feel good that he had taken the time to remember these feelings. Spain's history was important to him, and stopping by the museum allowed Javier to pay his respects to the past.

When Javier climbed into the boat each morning at Retiro Park, the calm of the small body of water astounded him. The stillness of the surrounding trees on all sides. The frozen stone sculptures and steps looming quietly. The day before it became a day, before loss and fear and worry could possibly descend upon it. As he propelled his small boat across the water, a feeling of endless tranquility poured into his body underneath the rising sun with the air still cool and birds just waking up in the trees. It was a feeling so perfect, so completely in harmony with the universe, that he couldn't possibly imagine anything in the day ahead that could change it. He couldn't imagine that the world could ever grow dark, and he thought this must have been how the people of Guernica felt before their village was destroyed. Their little town had no reason to be a target. There was no military base in Guernica, no advantage to be gained by opposing forces except fear and shock and intimidation. Guernica was merely a terrifying message, sent from those in power by way of the dismemberment of the innocent, the limbs of mothers and children blown to bits beneath the endless skies of Basque Country in the north of Spain. Alone in his boat each morning, feeling the beauty of life course through his veins, Javier was not so different from the people of Guernica before the bombings—trusting in his surroundings, comfortable with the beauty his eyes absorbed, and wholly unaware of what the future held.

When Javier looked at the sketches of *Guernica*, he couldn't stop thinking about how the most subtle changes impacted the entire composition. He thought Picasso was a brilliant painter, and he enjoyed contemplating what Picasso might have been thinking as he evolved the piece of art over time. It was a statement, but it was also art, and it seemed the more Picasso detached himself from his first emotions upon hearing the news of the bombing, the more powerful the piece of art became. It offered a more objective viewpoint, and it illustrated some of the cold, hard truths of the worst of humanity—illuminating the impersonal disregard humans could have for one another when they felt justified. Javier liked to look at these small panels. He liked to look at the panels and imagine Picasso in his apartment in Paris when he received the news. He liked to think of the rage and the tears and the transformation of emotion into art, of a moment into the momentous, of helplessness into hope. This is what he saw when he looked at the progression. He saw hope that the artist can only summon through great suffering. Hope that rises, like an arm from the ashes, protruding from the rubble, reaching out as the world crumbles all around.

*Guernica* was, after all, about the prospect of hope, somehow, some way, deep in the future.

Now that Javier was an old man, his future was not nearly as long as his past. He knew this, and he thought about this as he rowed across the serene waters. He thought about this as he watched the sun rise from his boat. And he thought about it each time he said hello to the docent at the Reina Sofía.

It was a crisp fall day. He woke early and rowed as he did each day. On the way back from Retiro Park, Javier walked past the Prado Museum on the way to the Reina Sofía, past the statues of Velázquez and Goya, thinking of *The Third of May 1808* even though it was October. The Spanish painters knew death, understood death, he thought. Like Velázquez and Goya so many years before him, Picasso knew what it meant to experience fear, to be at the very end, and face the firing squad. He understood the terror one felt when there was nowhere left to run, when your luck had run out, and the wheel was about to stop. Yes, Spanish painters knew this better than anyone, he thought, and this was always apparent in their art.

At the Reina Sofía, Javier made his way toward *Guernica*. When he arrived in the room, there was a crowd of students there, who stood somewhat patiently while the elegant docent spoke to them about the painting. Javier watched as she pointed toward the canvas, the graceful curve of her arm still attractive, and her eyes filled with wonder as she shared her enthusiasm for the work with the students.

When she was finished speaking, she asked the students to take fifteen minutes in the room without saying a word and without glancing at their phones. Fifteen minutes to look and see and hear and feel *Guernica*, to smell the smoke wafting through the village after the attacks and hear the cries of mothers at the sight of their dead children. The students gazed forward at the wall, as she stepped behind them only to see Javier with his back to the canvas, his eyes traveling across the small sketches of *Guernica* on the opposite wall.

He just stood there plainly, with his back to the crowd of people, staring at the sketches, in a room with no windows, with the rain now streaming down the glass of the exposed elevators that flanked the building. He just stood there, arms behind his back, bent slightly at the waist, leaning his head closer to try and get a better look. It was then he noticed, out of the corner of his eye, that he wasn't the only one with his back to the painting. The docent was looking in his direction, with her back to the students and also the painting. For a moment they were the only two people in the room, along with Picasso that is, who would likely have approved. It was nothing more than a coy, knowing smile that a woman can only give when she is older than seventy and knows that time is running out. Javier knew this, and he liked to think he was a man who was always prepared. But he was not prepared for this. He was prepared to row his boat in the mornings alongside other old men, and he was prepared to walk to the Reina Sofía and look at *Guernica* in the afternoons. But he was not prepared for this. He was not prepared to hope, really hope, not now, at his age. Hope, for a man his age, could only place him on the brink of despair. Even death didn't summon fear so much as inevitability. Hope was different, and Javier didn't dare hope, not even here at the Reina Sofía before *Guernica* where Picasso had spilled his hopes so powerfully across the canvas.

He had been in wars and seen the faces of death and stared blindly into sunsets, but her gaze felt like a hundred pairs of eyes leveling themselves at him, knowing and devastatingly beautiful. He had seen her so many times before and been fine. Although her smile was disarming, it was sweet, and he had never been intimidated by it.

Moreover, he had always been ready for it, coveted it like the stars or the moon or the sea. Only now it felt different. And he wasn't sure if it was the painting or the room or the thought that only hours before he had been rowing in the most tranquil waters. Oh, those tranquil waters, quiet, where old men in boats set out each morning completely at home and unafraid.

He had no choice but to meet her eyes and stare back into them. There was no averting her glance. They were there, alone in a crowded room, with the students facing *Guernica*. They were there, just the two of them, with only their thoughts, their considerable years, and days gone by that hung like the cracked, worn edges of his mouth—dry and sick with worry. All he could do in the moment was bow respectfully in her presence, doff his cap, and saunter out of the room, breaking the silence of the students by whistling a tune so old that only the two of them had ever heard it before.

# THE BULLRING

We visited Granada in the spring, just before tourist season was in full bloom. It was a good time to see the city. The streets were lovely and quiet. It was beginning to warm up. The trees were once again flush with leaves and the painted colors warmed the buildings down every crooked alleyway. The mad, summer heat would soon arrive. Although the Sierra Nevada mountains were soaked in glorious greenery after the conclusion of the winter months, they no longer boasted beautiful white snow caps. Just the same, it was lovely.

Granada is one of those majestic cities that rises up out of the earth and ascends as if summoned by the divine—even for nonbelievers. The magnificent Alhambra Palace sits fixed atop a great hill and overlooks the valley where Isabella once rode horseback with an army of troops from Santa Fe before the last Moorish kingdom in Spain finally acquiesced to Catholic rule. The city drips with history and is home to the final resting place of Ferdinand and Isabella as well. The city has cultural claims too. Granada's favorite son, Federico García Lorca, was shot to death just outside the city and his words flow through the pores of the capital of the province. All of this lore provides Granada with a mythical quality few cities can equal.

It was exciting to be in Granada and be traveling with Ava. In truth, it was exciting to be anywhere with Ava. We walked arm and arm, wandered into charming cafes, and took in all the main sights. We were at that stage in a relationship where it was new enough to be filled with wonder but just old enough for us to begin to consider a future that included one another.

Ava had been in love before. I thought I had been in love before but realized I hadn't when I met Ava. The feelings I had for her instantly shattered my previous notions of love, and I knew she had a different hold on me. Not only did I want to be with her, but I didn't want anything else. She could make me forget about the entire world and exile my pain into darkness. In the shadow of those bleak, banished memories, we arrived in Granada, in

Andalucía—where olive groves roll gently across the hills, time stands still, and the sun seems like a million years. These same feelings could be summoned in me by Ava.

Ava was beautiful. She wasn't beautiful in the way tall, alien fashion models were beautiful. She didn't possess a giraffe-like neck and her waistline wasn't infinitesimal. She was beautiful in a dream girl next door kind of way, with red-brown hair, freckles that swam like lights across her pale white skin, and an athletic body that was toned and taut. Runway models had nothing on her, and I knew it.

Her smile was disarming. From the first moment we met, it put my restless soul at ease and almost provided me with something approaching faith. It let me know that the worst things I could ever imagine would be better if she was there and informed me that the good things wouldn't be nearly as good without her. She had brown eyes that were lit with an unmistakable glint that was more magic than mischief. And she could get wide-eyed in a way that reminded me that being an adult didn't mean being boring, that the world could still light up for you if you allowed yourself to be swept up (just a bit) in a touch of that reckless innocence that time erodes. Her beauty was summoned from within, and it flowed out of her like oxygen. I couldn't get enough of it. Yes, Ava was beautiful, impossibly beautiful, and I walked ten feet tall when she was on my arm.

Although Ava was eight years older than me, she looked younger. My soul seemed more aged and battered, where hers still had wings. It was boundless, on a journey that would never end, filled with the type of buoyancy you see in the face of a small child the moment they go down a slide for the first time. A feeling that could only be uncovered amidst the immortality of exhilaration. That was Ava.

Since Ava was older than I was, she told me that I would have to get up to speed quickly. When I arrived late to the restaurant for our first date, she was already eating. "I know I am fast," she said, "but please try to keep up." Even if I was a natural, my learning curve would be steep. If a family was in my plans, she laughed without joking, I had better be ready to accelerate the timetable. She also informed me that if it took me more than twelve months to determine I wanted to spend the rest of my life with her, she'd already be gone. Truth be told, it only took me about twelve minutes, but I simply nodded and tried not to appear overanxious.

Spain was our third date. It was mad and impulsive. It was our third date, and it was as far away as possible. Far away from everything we had known, from the experiences we had previously had. It defied reason and logic, and we dropped everything to set out for the Iberian Peninsula. We didn't give it a moment's thought—consequences be damned. People we knew cautioned us against such an ambitious undertaking, to no avail. Nothing was harder than traveling, they said. Traveling overseas was even more daunting, they warned. But we felt something between us that was incapable of responding to reason, and we refused to let rational thought instruct something much more natural. It was almost as if we both possessed a keen awareness that, if we even considered reason for an instant, the moment would pass. And so, we set out for Spain.

Being in Spain felt like time travel. It was my first time traveling to Europe as an adult, and it seemed ironic to look back into history as we were in the process of creating our future. Perhaps we looked back for instructions or pitfalls or some sense of how to make the right choices and leave something permanent at the end of the day. Spain's history is not merely found in ancient buildings, but equally apparent in ancient traditions. Spanish people seem to have evolved less than people in other European countries. Or perhaps they merely hold their history more sacred. Either way, we felt a conscious resistance to progress that seemed both naive and admirable.

In the mornings, we would wake in our small hotel and look out over the red rooftops. We would look out at the red rooftops that spread themselves across the landscape like a blanket. We would look at them before the day had fully begun and listen to the birds chirping playfully from a tree in the plaza below.

I loved to look at Ava in the morning, before she put on makeup in an effort to look younger. She was already beautiful, but she was at her best in the morning, when her hair was splayed imperfectly across the pillow and the lines that were beginning to appear on her face were most visible. She would reach for my hand beneath the crisp white sheets and say nothing. She would lock her fingers inside mine and simply breathe, with her eyes closed, morning upon us, the birds calling outside our window, and the sun warming the room. There was nothing she could possibly do to enhance the beauty she displayed at this moment, and no mirror would ever be able to capture the sheen that rowed across her face at daybreak with her hand intertwined with mine and another twenty-four hours before us. Ava was unconvinced that this was the pinnacle of her beauty, that this was as high as one could ascend, but I knew better.

By the time we walked outside and stepped into the streets, Granada had awoken. Since it was springtime, the school year was still in full swing, and we enjoyed watching the children walking in their school uniforms each morning. The youngest children wore what looked like art smocks and they were adorable. The older children were dressed in polo shirts, skirts and pants and dress shoes and looked very well put together. It was quite an impressive ensemble.

We noticed the youngest children were often accompanied by fathers, and we were surprised by the number of men taking their children to school in this patriarchal country. "I like seeing the dads with their kids," said Ava. "It's nice."

We walked to the center of the city to see the cathedral. Inside the holy building, we sat and marveled at the tremendous girth of the marble pillars, which looked more like sequoia trees. Although neither of us were religious, we sat in the pews, stared upward at the monstrous dome, and paid homage to El Greco's paintings. "I can see why Catholicism was such a powerful force," I said.

The scope and scale of the achievement were immense and awe inspiring. It didn't seem possible that something so glorious could possibly have been built on the backs of men. There was a divine quality to the cavernous construction that embodied both the Renaissance and the Reconquista.

We had lunch near the cathedral and then returned to the apartment for a siesta. Andalucía continues to employ the siesta. Stores close their doors and bring down aluminum shades in the afternoon. Restaurants stop serving food and people generally head indoors to escape the heat of the day and rest. Most everyone in the streets during siesta is a tourist who can't quite figure out what to do with themselves. We didn't want to appear like tourists, so we headed inside to lay down. It was just as well, since we were still adjusting to the time change. We were tired, and we drew the blinds and then closed our eyes until we woke up when the sky was dark.

Ava felt rested and said, "Let's head out for tapas!" In Granada, restaurants and bars still serve a free tapa with every drink that is ordered. We both ordered glasses of red wine. Ava loved red wine. I didn't love it, but Ava did, and I tried to develop a taste for it. I realized my palate was less sophisticated, but we were in Spain. We were drinking wine and eating tapas in Spain al fresco style at a table pulled out into an old stone street in Granada under the night sky.

"I am very excited for tomorrow," said Ava. "The bullfights will be very exciting."

"Yes," I concurred, with some hesitation. "The bullfights should be exciting. They say the sun will be unusually hot tomorrow for this time of year, and the matadors will be very warm in the Andalucían sun."

There was a time when I wanted nothing more on earth than to see the bullfights. I read every Hemingway novel I could find, and I wanted to see the bullfights in Spain. I had seemingly already traveled the country, with Hemingway, as he followed the great matadors he befriended. *Death in the Afternoon* and *The Dangerous Summer* became like old friends, connecting me to tradition, culture, bravery, and a level of masculinity to aspire to. Bullfighting, in Hemingway's capable hands, was both sport and art, life and love, revelry and shame—wrapped in a linguistic romanticism. I became enamored with the most subtle movements of matadors, moved by the ceremony and pageantry, and awed by the courage summoned in the face of being gored. Those matadors! Those majestic, stylish, charming, dashingly handsome matadors!

Ava was excited to see the matadors too. "Have you noticed they are all so good looking?" she laughed.

\*\*\*

The bullfight began with a bit of pageantry, but it felt superfluous—more like a clumsy stultification of what all of the people had gathered for and were waiting to ensue. Once the bull ran into the ring, everything changed.

Ava didn't like the beginning of the bullfight when the focus was squarely on tiring the bull out. She didn't enjoy seeing the bull outnumbered, and she was fearful of the horses being injured or worse. The sun was hot, and the horses galloped lethargically, but they survived. The true depth of their suffering, of course, was unknown to us, circling the ring in the hot sun, and they did absorb some blows.

"This doesn't seem fair," said Ava.

"I am not sure bullfights are meant to embody fairness," I responded dully.

However, after a few minutes that seemed like much more, there was the matador, alone in the ring with the bull. Alone in the hot sun, with the jewels on his clothing glistening beneath the Spanish sky. Alone in front of thousands of fans, staring down the bull, with the sweat pouring out of his body, seeping into the fabric, and increasing the weight of his clothing.

For a moment, time seemed to stand still. The bull had already begun to tire, and he now slowed and sized up the matador. He appeared to catch his breath and measure the distance to the man before him. At the same time, the matador slowed his movements after the initial roars of the crowd. He seemed to check his feet, almost to ensure they were not embedded in the dirt and that they were capable of sauntering delicately, like a ballet dancer, once summoned. It is only a fraction of a second's time, but lifetimes pass, are considered, and the sun burrows down into the bullring. Yes, the sun is the best matador as Hemingway said. In Spain, in the south, in the late spring and early summer, the sun was even more formidable, and it only makes sense to acknowledge this. Ava leaned forward. I heard her take a deep breath. She looked at the matador in the hot sun. She watched the bull pull the dirt back and begin to charge forward, and I wasn't sure she even knew I was sitting next to her anymore. She slid forward toward the edge of the old wooden bench that supported us.

The bull was very powerful. He was powerful, and he thundered forward toward the matador. Ava gasped, but the matador was very calm, and he was very experienced. He was one of the best matadors in the world, and he seemed tranquil, moving elegantly in the hot sun. He made no sudden movements. His pace never changed, and it appeared as if an orchestration was taking place. The tempo was his, the conductor of the symphony. He worked very close to the bull, dangerously so, and Ava placed her right hand over her heart. The bull charged, over and over. Despite the spell that had been cast, he kept coming, lowering his horns, and propelling himself forward to whatever end awaited him. In the hot sun, he remained unrelenting. His will was unwavering. For as easy as the matador made things the look, the bull's movements were in stark contrast. They were the result of heart and fortitude rather than art and teachings. They were the offspring of indomitable will, labored, instinctual, working against the odds under the hot sun.

Even when the blood flowed and soaked the great animal's torso, he remained steadfast. The people cheered. His nobility was recognized, while the matador continued to dance to the same rhythm and Ava remained breathless.

I always wondered what could make a man stand in front of a bull. What could possibly make him confront life and death time and time again when mine was so precious to me? I couldn't understand the gravitational pull of the danger, the weight of generations of bullfighters in a single family, or the tradition that ran through this country's blood. Although the scales were tipped in the matador's favor, every matador had felt the horns of the great animal at some point, the animal they admired most, their only worthy adversary. They had absorbed his sharp point, almost invited it to pierce the surface of their skin and plunge into the body. This, of course, was inevitable, and yet the matador continued to forage, to pursue his calling, and perfect his art. On the morning of every corrida, he wakes up with the sun pouring in the window, a different sun than the one that will fill the bullring later, wondering if it will be his last. He wakes wondering, considering, perhaps even worrying, and he gets dressed, fastens the buttons of his glistening clothes, and stands before the bull and all the world, knowing this, feeling this, and yet somehow willing, resolved to give himself over to it. Magnificent.

I sat in the stands. I sat on the hard benches and watched Ava. I watched her body inch forward toward the edge of the seat. I saw beads of sweat emerge from her body and drip down her white skin, fall slowly, beautifully between her breasts. I saw her chest rise and fall, and I heard the vulnerable sounds escape from her body as the bull charged, the matador worked meticulously, and the sun beat down upon us. And when the matador leveled the bull with the blow that would finish him, she leaned into me. She leaned in forcefully, tenderly, brought her hands to her face, and she cried what seemed like ten thousand tears when the bull fell to the ground and the earth shook.

It was then that I knew, that I understood what it meant to be called by a force so strong, to be summoned by something that shatters everything in a man's head that is rational or practical or makes even a shred of sense. It was a feeling of powerlessness and empowerment all at once. To have a purpose so clear that it could defy all reason, that it could sweep every lesson taught into a wild abyss and turn the world on its head. It was hopeless, so spectacularly hopeless. It was hopeless, and I was happy. I was happy to feel hopeless, to feel my heart inside my chest, to feel the blood cut off from my brain in such a primal way.

Although I was still young, I had been waiting to feel this way all my life. All my life, I had been waiting to feel this, this feeling of what it felt like, not to think, but to know. I had always wondered how on earth a matador could ever summon the courage to stand before those bulls, feet in the dirt, motionless before the bull when the very act was an affront on human beings' basic instinct for self-preservation. I was no matador, but now I knew. I knew and it felt good to know what could make a man do something like that. It was a compulsion so strong that it preyed upon the most savage instincts a man can possess, and I knew that I would only ever stand in front of a bull … for her.

# THE GIN CLUB

In Sevilla, there is a gin club in the town center. It has a large, glass window facing the street. The window is very clean. It is very clean, and it reveals elegant furniture you might expect to find in the lobby of a five-star hotel. Here, luxurious couches and plush, old chairs surround handsome, low tables that are the absolutely perfect height to rest a drink. The low tables have glass tops with wrought iron legs, and old men sit around them and drink gin.

The Gin Club has a small, inconspicuous bar at one end of the room, but people don't sit at the bar. Only rarely is someone ever spotted sitting at the bar. They sit at the tables, and waiters in tuxedos take drink orders. They take drink orders from the menus on the tables, and they accommodate any drink so long as gin is the primary ingredient. This is a gin club, after all, facing the street in one of Spain's most beautiful cities, not far from the largest cathedral in the world.

The old men went to The Gin Club each Monday. They put on fine dress clothes and showed up faithfully, rain or shine, in every season of the year. Weather might have forced them to wear a topcoat or a newsboy cap from time to time, but they never sacrificed their dress code for the elements. Their dress code was their calling card, and it was important to them to live up to the standard they had set for themselves and for one another. Their loyalty to dignity through style was uncompromising.

Each of the old men liked to walk. In Spain, this is very common. Old men go for walks. They go for walks every day. They leave their small apartments, dressed to the nines, and take to the streets to stroll at their own pace. They stroll, sometimes with one arm behind the back, the other perhaps holding a cane, as they walk down the boulevards beneath old trees, in the shadows of the city. They frequently wear neckties, and you will never see them wearing a shirt without buttons. Theirs is not so much a quest for dignity, but rather an emphatic statement for having already achieved it. They drip in real class that has less to do with money than masculinity, and there is an unmistakable air about the old men in Spain that can only be classified as regal. It's inspiring and humbling, and the old men who met at The Gin Club each week embodied this ethos to the core.

Once the men entered The Gin Club, they were received at the door by Gerard, the man who took their coats and scarves. Gerard made sure the coats and scarves were secure, hanging them up carefully in the coatroom in the back, while the old men made their way to their table. They liked to sit at the table on the back wall, away from the large window but facing it. This provided them with the opportunity to see the street scene, but it also kept them relatively well cloaked, at the far end of the room, set against the dark, cherrywood walls of The Gin Club. That was just how they liked it. They liked to come to The Gin Club on Monday mornings and sit in the back of the room and drink gin. Most people don't drink gin in the morning. But old men, dressed impeccably, sitting together on plush sofas and chairs, can certainly drink gin in the morning. They can drink gin in the morning, in the company of friends and easy conversation, with the quickening world outside and their youth little more than a distant memory.

Francisco lived the furthest from The Gin Club. He had moved out of the center of town some years ago, and he traveled into the center by train. The train was very good in Sevilla, and he liked to take the train on Mondays. His wife worried that he might slip and fall getting off the train, but he told her not to worry. Francisco always told her not to worry, and she always worried. She always worried, like she had from the day they were married to the time they became parents until their son left the house and on and on. She would always worry, and Francisco would always tell her not to.

Once Francisco stepped off the train in Sevilla, he could feel the pulse of the city. Sevilla was tranquil and beautiful, but it was also vibrant. Although it was an old city, it afforded itself a youthful vibe, and Francisco could feel this. It reminded him of his youth, and he liked to see the young people moving freely with unencumbered limbs and laughing as if they would always be young. They lacked a complete awareness of what it would be like to age, and Francisco thought this was good. This unawareness allowed them to be young without fear of growing old, without contemplation of its constraints, and without the inevitable sadness that accompanies aging. He liked to see people without that sadness.

Unfortunately, Francisco had known sadness for many years. He been sad for a long time. He had been sad since the day their son died in a car accident. He was their only child, and he was a beacon of light. It would never disappear, the hole, the sadness, and he didn't want it to. It was just there, like a hundred-ton weight on his soul— never to be removed. People often asked him how he dealt with the loss. How did he and his wife go on? "You don't," said Francisco. "You don't ever go on. Not really. Not the same. Not ever. You just pretend to go on because there is no other choice." Every Monday morning, Francisco went to The Gin Club, and he didn't ever talk about his son.

Sergio was ageless, or so it seemed. Now in his eighties, he remained dashingly handsome. He still possessed a full head of hair, now silver, that he slicked back like Al Pacino or Anthony Quinn. He grew his hair longer than men his age were usually able to get away with, and the silver locks stood out against his bronze skin. He could often be seen driving through town in his old Alfa Romeo, the top down, sunglasses fastened carefully, with his long hair flowing behind. If there were any doubts that a man could age with style, Sergio quickly put them to rest.

He stayed in remarkable shape too—frequenting the gym daily and going on long bike rides outside the city center. Unlike Francisco, Sergio lived right in the heart of the city. He had a small villa in the country, but he rarely spent time there anymore. After all, he was alone, and he didn't like to feel lonely. He liked his small flat near the Alcazar. It was on the second floor, above the street level, but still only one flight of stairs for him to climb. The flat had a small kitchen, a sitting room, exceptional light, and a modest balcony that looked out at the glorious old city. When Sergio returned home, he liked to sit out on the balcony and watch the young people moving toward the night, toward their dreams, toward whatever future awaited them. He liked to look at the people, and he liked to move among them.

Sergio was one of those men that never married. He was built for bachelorhood. And unlike some friends of his who were now married for the second (or fourth) time, he knew it. The Catholic Church might have frowned upon him slightly, he surmised, but not nearly as much as those who were sworn to each other before God only to divorce some years later. That was a much greater sin, he imagined, than living alone, dating women half his age, and having multiple lovers throughout his lifetime. Sergio was who he professed to be, and he made it a point never to make promises he couldn't keep. If a woman stayed over on Sunday night, he let her know he would be leaving in the morning. He was not married, and he had no children, but he was loyal to Mondays and meeting his friends at The Gin Club. Sergio was not a man who liked to be confined by commitments, but he was fiercely loyal to the ones he had made. And if he went so far as to make a commitment, it would surely be kept.

Manuel wasn't born in Sevilla. He was from the North, and he grew up in Pamplona—home to the San Fermin Festival each year, Cafe Iruña, and the ghost of Ernest Hemingway. The North was different, and it had been his home for many years until he met a woman on holiday in Mallorca. She was a vision, the kind of woman who needn't speak to say much. She communicated primarily with her eyes and her smile. Her gaze was more than enough to disarm him, and their romance moved quickly. She grew up in the South, in Sevilla. Her parents lived in Sevilla and so did her two sisters and her three brothers. It was decided that Manuel too would live in Sevilla, that they would live in Sevilla, and that they would raise their family in Sevilla. From the day they met,

Manuel was certain this was his destiny. He had now lived in Sevilla for more than fifty years.

Sometimes, when the summer months arrived, Manuel dreamed of Pamplona, if only for a few days. He thought of the people from around the world who descended on his home and celebrated it. He thought of the streets he played on as a child, and he dreamed of watching the bulls tear through the narrow corridors with unimaginable, unstoppable force. They ran with such reckless abandon, unaware of their age, their mortality, and, of course, their fate. Manuel loved this about the bulls. There were times he wanted to tell them of what awaited them, but he didn't dare. They were perfectly savage and brave, unlike men, and he loved this about them.

Their life in Sevilla began with a sweeping, magical quality that seemed to complement their courtship. Angelina and Manuel had six children, four girls and two sons, and they raised them in the Andalucían capital. Her brothers and sisters had children, and their family grew large and strong.

When Manuel thought about these days when their children were young, they didn't seem real. He wasn't sure they had even happened. And he had to pull out old photos to confirm the accuracy of his memories, which seemed to vanish like a dream. Most everything had vanished since she died unexpectedly. The only saving grace was that it was quick, but she took everything with her. That hypnotic gaze, that first captured Manuel, left the world with his memories, his dreams, and ultimately … his heart.

That was now thirty years ago, and he had walked through the past three decades in something of a hypnotic fog, reaching, searching for remnants of Angelina throughout the city of her birth. He had thought about leaving and returning to the North, but his children and his grandchildren were in Sevilla. He wanted to be close to them, and he wanted to honor Angelina. The best way he could do that was through his loyalty to Sevilla and his undying love to everything she held dear. He took walks to Plaza de España, where he had proposed, and he went to the cathedral to pray multiple times a week. He wasn't religious, but he still went. He would sit down in the pews, enveloped by the massive building, and pray—to God. She had prayed to God when he did not believe. She had prayed to no avail and now he would too. He would sit there by himself and pray multiple times a week. But, on Mondays, he always went to The Gin Club.

Augustín lived a charmed life. He and his wife had been married for fifty years. They were healthy, and they had two children and five grandchildren. Their children were fine people, and they lived close by. They lived close by, and Manuel saw them often. They also had a number of friends and were a well-known couple around town. Augustín had been a successful business owner in Sevilla, and they had enough money to live out their lives very comfortably. By any measure, life had been good to them.

Augustín couldn't complain, but everyone has disappointments. Nobody can go through this world unscathed, and Augustín was no different. Despite the number of things that had gone well for him in his adult life, he lived the entirety of it with the knowledge that his own parents had died young and that they never had the opportunity to meet Augustín's wife and his children. They hadn't lived long enough to see Augustín become a success in business, and they had missed the vast majority of his life in general. This was a huge disappointment for Augustín, and he could never make peace with it. Time did nothing to heal this wound. He was eventually able to accept that this was reality, but he could never really accept that this reality was acceptable. It was cruel and savage and sat there over his entire life like a gaping void that only seemed to widen with the years.

Each Monday morning, he got up and moved his way to the dresser to select the clothes he would wear to The Gin Club. He could feel his wife watching him, as she always did, while he selected what he would be wearing that day. He wasn't known for his style, but he had listened to his wife for many years and had become better at putting an outfit together. He looked forward to this, and each Monday he tried to do something just a little different with the clothes he wore. There were many things about his life (most good) that he could not change, particularly at his age. But his clothes could be altered, shifted, and ultimately born again. This made Augustín feel like a new man, not a young man perhaps, but a new one, still capable of surprising people when so much of life seemed scripted and predetermined at this point. Once he had dressed for the day, he ate a small breakfast at home, just enough to coat the lining of his stomach, and walked out the door to catch a bus to The Gin Club.

On Monday mornings, The Gin Club was empty. In fact, when it first opened, the owner hadn't even considered extending the hours to the morning. Gin was to be consumed in the evenings, after the sun had been lowered and the sky grew dark. An argument could have been made that a nice gin and tonic was also appropriate in the afternoon, a refreshing cocktail combatant against the steamy, Andalucían sun. But morning? That was a stretch, and it wasn't until the old men approached Teo that he even considered it.

Teo (short for Mateo) was a middle-aged man, who still looked young. He was in his early forties but looked as if he was a decade younger. He had a full head of hair without a single streak of gray, and his toned, tan skin might have made him out to be a surfer if he didn't wear a business suit so well. But he always wore a business suit, the finest business suits, complete with a handkerchief and cufflinks—the little things that added a touch of class to an outfit. The old men noticed this. They noticed the little things, and they noticed that most men Teo's age weren't in touch with them. Young men didn't care about the details. They couldn't be bothered by the small touches, the finishing touches, the extra mile. But Teo was different. He was young and modern, but he was a throwback, an example of days gone by, and he never missed an opportunity to tip his cap to the past. The old men loved this about him.

"Teo," Sergio called out to him one evening. "The boys and I were thinking. Would you ever consider opening The Gin Club in the morning?"

Teo looked at Sergio and the other old men. He was surprised, but he thought about the question carefully. The men could tell he was giving it his full consideration.

"Well, …" he said. "I am not really sure that it would be profitable, that we'd be able to attract customers. I am open to anything, but we cannot survive without customers."

The men looked at each other for a moment. This wasn't their first rodeo, and they had discussed things beforehand. It had been easy to predict that Teo might meet their question with some resistance, but they had also predicted correctly that he would be open to the possibilities.

"We understand, Teo," said Manuel. "Would you consider opening in the morning just one day a week. The four of us will commit to being here, and we will order four drinks apiece."

"And we will cover the cost of you, Gerard, the bartender, and any additional staff for the entire time," added Augustín. "You will just need to cover the cost of the electricity, Teo." Sixteen drinks of your finest gin should suffice."

Teo nodded, impressed. He nodded again, and he thought about the proposal. Monday mornings were usually spent at home with his wife, following the weekend, after their children went to school. He would have to discuss this with her, but he liked the old men. He liked the old men very much, and he wanted to be able to open The Gin Club for them, just for them, on Monday mornings at the start of the week.

And so, this was how Monday morning came to be the time the four men met each week. When you are old, it's just the opposite of being young when it comes to your schedule and the days of the week. Predictably, weekdays are often slow with little to do, and old men must work exceptionally hard to remain busy. Weekends are just the opposite—drenched in activities with children and grandkids—or women in Sergio's case. It was both rewarding and exhausting. The men enjoyed the rewards, but they were tired. By Monday morning, they were ready to relax, and beginning the week with gin, while the young people moved steadily past the window on their way to work, was the perfect way to do this. They would often arrive only to collapse into the plush upholstery. Teo would always come over to say hello with the same words each week. "Tough weekend, gentlemen?" he would ask.

"Yes," said Sergio emphatically. "Didn't you see Sevilla play on Saturday?"

Sevilla's *fútbol* team was both an inspiration and a constant source of frustration. They were good, very good, and they had won the Europa League multiple times in recent years. But they were still inferior to Real Madrid, Barcelona, and Atlético Madrid. They were good enough to come tantalizingly close to challenging for trophies in Spain without quite being able to deliver. This past weekend they had suffered a tough defeat at the hands of Valencia. Sevilla FC was a good club that constantly lived in a special purgatory reserved for the almosts, what ifs, and could've beens.

"We need more talent up front," said Francisco. "We won't compete with the best if our side is filled with castoffs from other clubs."

"It is true," reiterated Manuel. "A team of mercenaries will never get the best of Barcelona. We must build through the academy and manage to keep the best young players."

"Like Sergio Ramos," chimed in Augustín. "What I wouldn't give to have had him anchoring the back line all these years."

"Gentlemen," said Sergio, requesting their attention. "You are living in a fantasia, as these things will never happen. Each week, we come here and discuss the team, but we will never be the equal of Madrid or Barcelona. On a given day, we may compete with them. On a given day, we may beat them, but we will never be their equal. We are Sevilla, beautiful Sevilla, with a glory all our own. Why do we need to be anything else but that?

"*Vale*, Sergio," Francisco acquiesced. "*Vale*. How old is she? Please tell us. Each week, you come in here walking on air after parking your sports car, with your hair slicked back and not a care in the world about the shoddy defense Sevilla has played during the weekend. Please. How old is she this time? You must tell us."

"If you must know," Sergio remarked in dignified fashion, "she is forty-eight years old. So, you can't make the argument in this case that I am not thinking straight or that my judgment is clouded or that my vision is not true."

"Need I remind you that you are eighty-one years old, Sergio?" said Manuel calmly. "She may not be twenty-eight, but she is, after all, still thirty-three years your junior."

The other men laughed. They laughed in the quiet room, on the plush couches with the taste of gin in their mouths. It was good for them to laugh, and they came here to laugh. After all, life was hard, even for those who lived the most charmed lives. They came here to detach from those parts, to forget, perhaps not to drown their sorrows in a glass but, at the very least, to disappear in a sea of lighthearted humor, bad jokes and gentle teasing for a few hours.

But Sergio was not laughing. This time he was serious about Sevilla and about the woman he was with the night before.

"I do not know what my age is," he said with a straight face. "And I don't wish to be reminded of it. Have you heard that saying, 'How old would you be if you did not know how old you were?' It is a very true statement, and I do not feel as if I am very old. Moreover, I won't pretend to be, and I see no point in accelerating the race to the finish line where only a grave awaits."

"But we are old," remarked Augustín. "We are old men who have been around for many years. That is why we are here, at The Gin Club, on a Monday morning, because we are old. We are here because we are old men and old friends who have been around long enough to see the world run by men who are much younger than us."

Sergio didn't say a word. He just looked out, past his friends, toward the big window and the street outside. He looked out at the young people walking past on their way to work. He looked out, past the years and disappointments and the coatroom, which held their belongings. He enjoyed coming to these weekly gatherings because they were lighthearted and breezy. The old men were friends, old friends, and they usually shared quite a few laughs and generally kept the world at bay, kept life, real life, at a distance where none of them could really see it unless they were looking. The old men liked this, for a few hours. They liked to talk *fútbol*. They liked to think about what Sevilla's team needed to compete for La Liga. It mattered very little if this was a "fantasia," so long as they could talk about it, dissect it, and dream of things that would never happen. Furthermore, *fútbol* made for safe conversation that was the perfect companion to gin in the morning.

The old men had known each other long enough that there were no secrets. They had witnessed births and baptisms and had buried more family members than they cared to recall. Each was keenly aware of the other's great disappointments, their losses, and they understood that there were some things in life you never come back from. You may go on, but you never come back.

Each man understood this, and they made sure never to discuss any of these things on Mondays. On occasion, they might have confided in one another in private, but Mondays were sacred. Regardless of how much weight they were carrying, the banter on Monday mornings was meant to offload, to escape, and generally to isolate the old men from the hard truths of reality—if only for a moment. Gin was merely the coating that lined the stomach and, more importantly, the heart, before it would once again process the day, the week, and whatever years they had ahead.

The old men were very committed to this approach, which is why it was so out of character that Sergio broke rank that Monday morning. He was always good-natured about the jokes that frequently centered around the age of the women he dated. In some ways, he wore it as a badge of honor, and he certainly didn't shy away from it. He expected it, accepted it, and it was unlike him to become so defensive. Nothing ever seemed to strike a raw nerve with him. Nothing stuck, and Sergio might have looked like a pretty boy, but he was like iron. He was tough as nails, and this was one of the things his friends admired about him.

As soon as Teo noticed the old men were nearly done with the first round, he walked over to the table and asked them what they were going to go with next.

"*Puerto De Indias Fresas* gin and tonic please, Teo," said Manuel. This was a local gin that had recently become popular. On the surface, it could have appeared less masculine—with a sweeter taste and a pink hue. However, the gin was from Sevilla. It was from Sevilla, a city draped in warm colors, and the men liked to drink Puerto de Indias. They took pride in it, and fruit seemed to go along well with breakfast anyway.

"Very well," said Teo, noticing that the men were unusually quiet this morning. He had come by the table in the wake of Sergio's reaction and sensed the slight tension among the men. "Can I get you anything else?" he inquired politely but unobtrusively.

"No, thank you, Teo," said Sergio. "That's all. *Todo bien.*"

The men continued to drink their gin. They drank their gin just as they always did, a little quieter this morning, but still drinking. Truth be told, each man usually took his drink with two personas, caught between two worlds, no matter how hard they tried. Francisco hoisted a silent toast to his late son, and Manuel acknowledged his sweet wife when he pulled the glass to his lips. Augustín made sure to tip his cap to his dad, the man who had gone far too soon, who liked to take a drink of gin at the end of the day. The old men never talked about these silent acknowledgments, but they were there. The unspoken presence of the dead always are. All except Sergio, who toasted to life, to love, to the many women he had been with, and to the endless Spanish roads in the countryside that caressed his Alfa Romeo. He toasted Sevilla and the *fútbol* team, eating grapes to ring in the New Year at Plaza Nueva, and he toasted the splendor of Andalucía bathed in olives and now gin.

Although Sergio may not have toasted his own existence, he always made a silent toast to his friends, to their incredible resolve, and to their ability to come here each week and get together. He was grateful that it was important to them, that they worked to conceal their pain for a few hours, and that they greeted him with a warm embrace. It was a pact they had made, and the old men honored it. They honored it, and they honored Sergio. He was their friend, their friend for so many years, and they knew that he wasn't nearly as wounded as they were. Sergio knew it too, of course, and he loved them for never letting on when he was well aware that they knew.

Earlier in the morning, Sergio had woken up in his small apartment. Anne had stayed over the night before, and he had watched her sleep in his bed, with the sheets furled around her and the morning light cascading through the window and catching the length of her body, her back exposed with light brown hair falling around her shoulders. She was lovely, perfectly lovely, and he liked Anne. He liked Anne very much, and he didn't want her to leave in the morning. Moreover, he didn't want to leave her, not even on Monday, with his friends waiting to meet him at The Gin Club.

Sergio had been seeing Anne for a few months. She was divorced, with two kids in their twenties, and she had moved to Spain after living in the UK. She was independently wealthy, having inherited a fortune from her father's textile business, and she didn't need a man in order to survive. She wasn't looking for one either when she ran into Sergio and his smooth bravado while shopping for vegetables at the market. He asked her to dinner, and the relationship grew from there.

The night before was the first time Anne had really asked Sergio about his family.

"So, you never married?" she said.

"No," said Sergio. "I never saw the point. So many restrictions. So many headaches. So many marriages that end in divorce."

"With that attitude," remarked Anne, "I can see why. You certainly seem to have had your mind made up."

"I am not sure if my mind was made up so much or if there was never anyone who came along and seemed to be able to change it," he said. "Deep down, I think I might have been more open than I projected, but it never happened."

"So, no siblings? No wives? No kids? Nieces? Nephews?" said Anne. "All these years. That is a long time to go without." Sergio thought carefully about Anne's remark. It was a long time, and he had been alone. He had always been alone.

"I suppose it is," said Sergio. "It is a long time. This is how I have lived my life."

"Is it lonely?" asked Anne. "Living with nobody in your life. Do you feel lonely?"

"At times," said Sergio. "At times, the loneliness is inescapable. Other times, it brings solace, comfort, and tranquility."

"I think it is sad," said Anne emphatically. "I think it is the saddest thing I have ever heard."

"Nobody should feel sad for me," said Sergio. "I made my own choices, and I live with them. In a sense, I live by them. There can be no real sadness when you have had the good fortune of being able to make your own choices. Regret possibly, but not sadness."

"Well, I think it is sad," said Anne. "Impossibly, terribly sad."

Sergio sat there, looking at Anne, trying to decipher the look on her face, the absolute strangeness she felt about the life he had led. They were outside, under a warm light, at a cafe near the center. Although it was Sunday evening, a few people were still out on the streets, walking under the pale moon. Sergio looked beyond Anne, just over her left shoulder, and into the blackness of the night. He looked farther and farther until his vision was inhaled by the dark sky.

"I watched my friends suffer," remarked Sergio painfully. "Suffer a lot. It wasn't easy. Their boats took on a lot of water over their lifetimes, and they lost a lot. They lost big, and they never recovered. I never wanted to suffer losses like that."

Anne sat there quietly, focused intently on each word he was saying.

"At times, it seemed like a cruel joke," he went on. "Their lives gave them so much joy, only to strip it away so savagely, to take it away so unapologetically, leaving scars behind that would never, could never, heal. I wasn't willing to give as much or go as far. I played some hands, but I always knew when to fold. I understood just how to escape before the money was gone. I have spent my life employing that strategy. It worked for me, and I never questioned it."

"Do you not have a soul, Sergio?" asked Anne. "And if so, what has nourished it?"

"I have a soul, like anyone else, but I am not sure it has ever been nourished, truly nourished, at least not in the sense you suggest," said Sergio. "But it has been comforted and it has soared on the wings of many nights spent in the company of beautiful women, the laughter of friends, and the adventure of new horizons, the next horizon, whatever exists just over the next rise. The promise of what comes next, what might come next, has provided meaning and a sense of hope—if not a genuine purpose."

A young couple sped by on a *moto*. The woman was on the back, wearing a pink helmet with her arms wrapped tightly around the man driving and her head turned and pressed against the back of his black, leather jacket. Both Anne and Sergio watched them carefully. They were young, and they rode with a fearlessness, an abandon, that was akin to youth. Their *moto* throttled between the old buildings, her golden hair flowing out from beneath the helmet as he leaned left and right navigating the corridors.

"You are happy with this life you have chosen?" asked Anne.

"Until recently," said Sergio. "I always thought I was happy with it until recently. Now I am having some doubts."

"You are an old man, Sergio," said Anne. "You can't be capable of learning new tricks at this stage."

Sergio hesitated. He wasn't sure he could articulate his feelings with the eloquence required, and he wanted to get the words right.

"Each Monday, as you know, I meet my friends at The Gin Club. We have known each other for many years, and it is my favorite day of the week. We never talk about anything painful or serious. The conversation is purposefully light, and we might discuss *fútbol* or travel or gin or our favorite movies or the best flamenco guitarists. Of course, we reminisce about some of the times we shared in the past. We sit and laugh and tell lies like all old men, about the good old days when we were young men, capable of doing the things that young men do. But the weight is always there, down deep, and I can feel it each time we meet, almost as if it is gaining ground."

"The weight?" said Anne. "What do you mean?"

"The weight of their experiences. The richness. The weight of life's loves and life's losses. As I said, we have an unspoken rule never to talk about these things, and they wouldn't dare. But they don't have to talk about them in public in order for the weight to be felt. We aren't the poker players we once were, and the spectacular pressure builds each week.

"How do you all manage this?" asked Anne, captivated now, and less judgmental.

Sergio paused. He took a moment to take a sip of his drink, place it back on the table, and lean in closer. He was now looking at Anne, almost looking into Anne, and she could feel the care with which he was preparing to choose his words.

"Usually, the conversations will be shifted to me. I am the one with the young girlfriends, the sports car, and my life makes it easy to elicit a laugh or bring the decibel level down. As our conversation disappears into my life's travails, they feign envy, but I know that's not really the case. They want me to feel good, to feel fortunate, and to feel their feigned desire to live vicariously through me. All I feel is their pity, like your sadness, and I have never wanted their pity."

They sat in silence for many minutes before Anne decided to speak. "Why don't you mention this to them?"

"Because … they are my friends, my dear friends. It's almost a brotherhood and, being the one who can infuse the conversation with humor, even at my own expense, is an easy price to pay in order to ease their pain, their long-suffering pain that subsides gently, slightly, temporarily in the wake of my escapades. Even their pity arrives with its own justification for the pain they feel, the lives they have led, and the terrible losses they have endured. I've simply never had enough, felt enough, or cared enough to be truly vulnerable, susceptible to the possibility of a great loss."

Anne didn't say a word. She just kept looking at Sergio, and she made sure not to look at him with sadness. In some way, she felt admiration, as what could easily be construed as selfish behavior, in some odd, twisted way, now seemed noble and generous. Sergio looked down slightly. He took out a cigarette, lit it, and didn't say a word. They sat at the outdoor table, and he crossed one leg stylishly over the other. They just sat, for what seemed like hours but was likely only minutes, until Sergio paid the bill, stood up, and offered Anne his arm. They walked home to his apartment, past the Alcazar, in the warm glow of the lights in Sevilla.

When they got home, Sergio poured each of them a drink, and he put on his favorite record. He stood up, offered his hand, and they danced cheek to cheek, with their bodies close until they went to bed. They went to bed in each other's arms until the sun rose over the great cathedral in Sevilla. Sergio woke up in the morning to go to The Gin Club while she slept. He couldn't be late, and he exited the apartment quietly, with the beautiful curve of her back once again revealed and her hair falling around her shoulders.

The old men sat around the table. They sat around the table and drank gin and didn't talk anymore about Sevilla's *fútbol* team. They sat on the plush couches and chairs. They sat together and didn't say a word. They sat while Teo went to bring them the check. It was nearly the middle of the day. The sun was high in the sky and they had consumed gin in the morning, in beautiful Sevilla, near the end of their lives that had been so long. They were together, but each man was left alone with his thoughts.

Sergio thought about Anne. He thought about her and her bewildered look the night before and her light brown hair and her exposed back and her probing questions. He thought about her in his apartment. He liked to think about her in his apartment, and he hoped she would still be there when he returned home.

"I have met someone," he announced to his friends for the first time in all their Mondays at The Gin Club. "I have met someone," he repeated. "Her name is Anne."

# THE CLEANEST ALIMENTACIÓN IN SPAIN

The *alimentación* was clean. It was clean and neat and had many things that people could buy. The shelves were filled with crisps, ramen noodles, dried cups of soup, and sauces including American ketchup. Inside the refrigerators, cans of soda were stacked neatly above chilled bottles of wine that people in Spain prefer to drink on warm days.

Behind the counter, there was a freezer with bags of ice packed perfectly to maximize every inch of space. In Spain, ice is like gold. It's rare and a real commodity in the Andalucían summers when the air gets thick and the temperatures rise. But the *alimentación* was clean, impeccably clean. It was neat and clean, and it was easy to see that everything was in its place.

Each morning, around nine thirty, María would arrive to open the *alimentación*. She would slide the metal garage door upward, revealing the large, glass window facing the narrow street. She would step through the doorway and enter the darkness that filled the store. She walked inside, placed her shoulder bag behind the counter and took quick visual inventory before even turning on the lights. She moved with purpose and precision. There wasn't a sense of urgency, but María possessed an attention to detail that wasn't always apparent with proprietors in Spain. She didn't look hurried, but she proceeded with a certain intent and focus that was undeniable.

Sometimes, when I entered to get a cold drink at the start of the day after an early morning walk, the lights were still off. The door had been opened, but the day's customers had yet to arrive. María would smile and say, "*Buenos días*," warmly. Over time, I had become something of a regular, and it almost seemed that María prioritized my arrival at the start of the day, often completing the transaction before even bothering to turn on the lights.

"*Uno ochenta,*" she'd say, and I would have my coins ready. Each time, she accepted my money, she did so with genuine appreciation, and I liked going there. I liked María. I liked her store, and it was nice to go there in the morning. She was always friendly, and it was nice to get a drink and be friendly. This was one of the things I liked most about Spain. People were friendly and they made the smallest interactions pleasant.

Like most of the *alimentación* owners in Spain, María was Chinese. Of course, María was just her Spanish name. Chinese business owners often adopted a Spanish name as a way to integrate with the locals, although it is unclear whether this approach was effective. They learned Spanish, and they opened their *alimentaciones* for business.

One day, I asked my friend Juan why no Spaniards owned or worked at *alimentaciones*. Although I admired the increased diversity in provincial Spain, I couldn't understand why no Spanish men or women operated these businesses. Juan replied that *alimentaciones* were open for more hours than other businesses. They began the day earlier, didn't close for siesta, and stayed open later into the evenings. Oh, and they worked Sundays too. "Spaniards," he said, "simply aren't willing to work as hard as the Chinese families who immigrate to Spain."

According to him, this was the reason no Spaniards had *alimentaciones*. María confirmed this work ethic one morning, sharing that her exercise was walking ninety minutes to and from work each day.

During the week, it seemed like María was always working in the *alimentación*. Sometimes with her husband. Sometimes alone. But she was there from the time the store opened in the morning until long into the night when people stumbled out of tapas bars and through the door in search of a piece of candy, soda, or bottle of water. Regardless of the condition of the patrons, María employed the same poise and kindness. This was their business after all. They were in a foreign country, and they worked hard to accommodate the local culture as it was. From day one, they understood they were playing the long game. Trust would take time, but they were willing to do whatever they could to become part of the community.

The *alimentación* was on a long street that ran from one area in the center of town to another. It wasn't a main thoroughfare, but it was an effective cut through for taxis and scooters. The street was mostly comprised of tapas bars and a *panadería*, which made it an attractive place for tourists, locals, and anyone traveling on foot. At the bottom of the street was a handsome plaza with great trees that rose into the sky and surrounded an impressive statue, which was the centerpiece. This allowed people to get something at the *alimentación* and then wander down to the plaza with their snack or drink in search of a bench, with the sun streaming in from all corners of the plaza, enveloping them in a warm embrace. I loved to bring my drink to the plaza with a book and take up temporary residence on an iron bench. But the *alimentación* was well located, surrounded by dozens of apartment buildings and easily available to residents and tourists alike.

In Spain, it isn't uncommon to enter an *alimentación* and see the smoke rising to the ceiling or inhale the stale stench of cigarettes permanently suspended in a small space. But María never smoked inside her *alimentación*. If she smoked at all, she made sure not to do it in her *alimentación*, and the air in her store smelled fresh. The floor was also smooth and clean. There were never any signs of footprints that had been there earlier in the day, and María made sure of this. She swept and mopped throughout the day to ensure that people felt like they were entering their own home.

On the shelves, the canned food and glass jars were lined up, the labels centered meticulously, facing directly toward the customer. When a customer would come in and handle an item on the shelf, María would make note of this. However, in an effort not to embarrass the customer or make them aware of her obsessive nature, she would wait until they had left the store. Then she would peek out from behind the register and walk around the counter. She would calmly turn the label back, centered perfectly once again for the next customer who might enter the store. This did not bother her. It did not bother her that customers handled the items, and it did not bother her to return them to their original position. It was simply what she did, a measure in place to maintain the cleanest *alimentación* in town.

On weekends, her son Jorge worked in the store in order to give María a break and allow her to spend time with her younger children. During the week, Jorge helped out with his brothers and sisters. He assisted them with their homework, made them dinner, and helped get them off to school. Jorge was eighteen now, in his final year of *Bachillerato* at a *colegio* near their apartment. He was an excellent student. He was very responsible. And he liked to help his mother. On the weekends, he did this by working at the *alimentación*. He was proud of his mother, and he liked the store. It was good to work at the store, and Jorge liked to help his mother out by working there over the weekend.

Jorge could move easily between, Spanish, English, and Chinese. Unlike María, who had command of two languages (Chinese/Spanish), Jorge had mastered three. He spoke each of them very well, and this was particularly helpful when interacting with tourists—many of whom came from the United States, United Kingdom, and China. Jorge was now learning German too and already knew a bit of Italian as well. This made him an asset in the store on Saturdays and Sundays when the volume of tourists increased. In fact, some English-speaking expats even waited until the weekend to purchase goods, since they knew Jorge spoke such good English.

Jorge was big for his age. Tall and big. A little overweight and not particularly athletic. He was the kind of kid who might be made fun of even if he wasn't Chinese. Being Chinese in Spain made things even harder, but Jorge was strong. His body was stronger than it might have appeared, and his internal fortitude exceeded his physical strength—which was considerable. His family had come to Spain when he was young, and he was used to people rolling their eyes or muttering under their breath.

Moreover, this wasn't simply Spain. This was Granada, in Andalucía, where the tradition is rich, the culture embedded, and the region extraordinarily provincial. Granada was far less diverse than some of the larger cities in Spain. This made things harder for a new family, an immigrant family, particularly when they were taking business from Spaniards in such a difficult economic time. Jorge knew these things. He understood, and he carried this understanding with him when he went to work in the store each weekend. He thought of his place in the world as he walked to the *alimentación*, and he wondered if things would always be this way. Times change, he thought. He hoped. Perhaps not as quickly in Spain as some other countries. But nothing stays the same. Not forever. Not the wars or the weather or the wind. Jorge wasn't holding his breath, but he had a degree of faith, and he would be ready when things were different.

One week after the conclusion of Semana Santa, the biggest festival in Granada, Jorge was working at the store on a Sunday when few places were open. A group of four boys his age walked into the *alimentación* without giving Jorge so much as an acknowledgement. One boy said something with his hand covering his mouth while the others laughed. Jorge knew they were likely talking about him as he stood quietly by the register. He was a little agitated, but he tried not to show it. He stood up as straight as he possibly could, and he tried to remain composed. It wasn't difficult for Jorge to remain composed. He was mature for his age, and he took it in stride.

"*Chino!*" said one of the boys. "*Mira,*" he called out as he took his left hand and swept a row of cans off the shelf, sending them tumbling to the floor while the other boys laughed. Jorge moved out calmly from behind the counter and toward the boys. He knew they were trying to rile him up. He stood in front of them inside the store. It was Sunday afternoon. The air was warm, and the light was streaming in. The streets were empty. There was nobody else around. It was just him and them, staring, basically eye to eye, although Jorge looked down on them slightly due to his height. The boys smiled, almost taunting Jorge, begging him to take a swing at one of them. Their eyes were laughing, waiting for Jorge to respond, to unleash his emotions, perhaps in the form of a clumsy, awkward punch in their direction.

As Jorge stood there in front of the boys, the long lens of history flashed before his eyes. This history of China. Of Spain. Of his ancestors. From the Great Wall to the

Alhambra Palace, where the Moors once reigned supreme before Ferdinand and Isabella conquered southern Spain. He thought of his parents, the distances they had traveled to arrive here, the sacrifices they had made for their children, the dignity with which they carried themselves. He thought of the twelve lions at the Alhambra, carved in perfect stone, frozen for eternity, that could not roar even at the most infuriating moments. He thought of these great lions most of all.

Whenever he was forced to bite his tongue or hold back his fists, he would focus on the lions. These lions had been there for centuries. They were handsome and strong and chiseled in stone. They guarded the beautiful court, looked out from the inside at the surrounding walls, and were confined for eternity with a presence but no voice. Jorge understood what the lions felt. He understood, and he knew what it felt like to be rendered speechless and still need to stand tall.

"*Perdone*," he said, as he moved past the boys only to reach down, pick up the cans, and return them to the shelf. He took his time with each one, reaching down carefully, grabbing them in his hand, and then lining the shelves with the labels facing out just as his mother would.

"*Nada?*" one of the boys said. "*Nada? Claro.*"

Jorge felt the anger rush through him from the inside. He wanted to wipe the smiles off their faces. He dreamed of shoving one of them against the wall and telling them not to come back. They had tried to humiliate him, and he felt the desire for some sort of retribution. But he knew that wasn't possible. His family had too much to lose, he thought. There would be other days. There would be other opportunities, different opportunities. But today was not that day. Jorge knew that and had to accept that his yearning for retribution would have to wait.

Jorge had been in Spain for the majority of his life, and in many ways he felt Spanish. He had been to Mirador San Nicolas when young couples would take photos after getting married in a nearby church. He liked to see the couples dressed up, the bride in a flowing white dress against the sprawling, stone backdrop of the Alhambra Palace and the groom dressed smartly in a dark coat alongside her. He had seen Spanish couples there, and he had been there when Chinese couples took photos as well. But he had never seen a couple from different backgrounds. This he had not seen, not once in all his trips to the mirador with the Alhambra in the distance and the great Sierra Nevada mountains peering over its ancient shoulder.

Her name was Lucía, and she was in Jorge's class. She was Spanish and she had long, dark hair and eyes that even seemed to shine on the darkest days. They lit up every room she entered, and Jorge waited each morning to see her walk through the door. Like Jorge, Lucía was a very good student, and he often found himself working alongside her at school. Jorge could tell by her eyes that she was kind. She was kind and understanding, and she never pitied him. Most of the Spanish kids at school either pitied him or resented him. Lucía did neither. Outside of class she always said a warm hello, even though her friends moved swiftly past Jorge as if he wasn't there.

By now, he was used to the cold treatment, but Lucía was different. She raised the temperature in the room, and she gave him hope. Hope for Spain. Hope for the future. Hope for himself. They shared a bit of an unspoken language, and Jorge wouldn't dare risk their quiet bond by revealing any deeper feelings he might have had. No, for now this was enough. This was more than enough. To dream was more than enough, and he looked forward to seeing her each day he went to school. He couldn't wait to be welcomed each morning by her smile. It was all that he needed in order to propel him through the rest of the day and into the weekend when he would work in the *alimentación* that his mother worked so hard to run all week long.

The boys in the store laughed in his face, collected a few items they wouldn't be paying for, and walked haughtily out the door. I just happened to brush by the boys on the street before I walked into the *alimentación*.

When I walked inside, Jorge had returned to his place behind the counter. He said a respectful hello, and he tried to stand as tall as he was able, gazing coolly, as the boys disappeared down the street. Once they were out of sight and out of earshot, Jorge tallied the items they had stolen on the register. He reached into his pocket, took out his own money, and processed the payment to eliminate any profit loss that would have been evident to his mother.

On Monday morning, María entered the *alimentación* in the dark as she did at the start of each week. The shelves were lined perfectly, with each label facing out, and there wasn't a speck of dirt on the floor. She checked the register and went over the books. The store had made a handsome profit over the weekend on the heels of the week following Semana Santa. Once again,

Jorge had done a fine job. He was a good boy, she thought. He was a good boy and he had done a good job. She turned on the lights, propped open the door, and waited to greet the first customer of the day. Moments later, I walked in.

# THE CLIFFS

I n the early morning, the cliffs were silent, and he could hear the waves rush gently to the shore. The birds had yet to take flight, and only a few sailboats had left the dock. It was nice and bright, and it was hours before kayaks would flood the bay with tourists.

He liked to walk each morning at this time of day. The air was still cool, and he liked it when the wind hit his face. It reminded him of a different time in his life, when he lived in a colder climate and the days weren't so perfect and endless. He liked to think of those days, when the air was crisp, and his dreams never left his small neighborhood. That was a long time ago.

When the wind whipped up, he had to be careful not to walk too close to the edge. In the country of his birth, there would likely have been a railing, but here, on the other side of the world, nobody was going to try and save you from your own stupidity. There were no signs and he was careful to keep a safe distance. After all, the wind doesn't play favorites.

Down below, the wet rocks spread out at the base of the cliffs and lined the small beach. They were smooth and dark from the sea and covered in emerald green moss. The emerald green moss was slippery, and it gleamed in the morning sun. The sand was wet and tight, and there wasn't a single footprint to be seen. He liked to come here in the mornings, to get close enough to the edge to see the untouched shore before it was trampled by feet.

He walked this route nearly every morning. Every morning he was able anyway. There were some mornings when his back refused to cooperate. Others when the soreness in his knee was too much. But he tried to walk this route every morning. The exact same route, with each step laid out just as it had been the day before. He never tired of the repetition. It did not bore him to take the same route over and over. It provided him with the relative certainty that the next day should be just as the one before.

The man had lived near the cliffs for a long time. He had a small apartment near the coast, and he liked to wake up with the sun. He liked the idea of starting the day as soon as it began and waking up with the sun made him feel as if he had done that. So, each night before he went to bed, he checked the exact time of the next morning's sunrise. This way he could set his alarm to synchronize with the start of the day.

His apartment was very small, but he liked it very much. He had a bed, a kitchen table, and a small living area. There were a few paintings on the wall and a small television propped on an old wooden stand. The floor was tile, and the flat had good light. It was important to have good light. Good light was more important than space, he thought. Space by itself was empty but light could fill any room. His apartment had good light, and the light filled the space perfectly.

There wasn't much to the flat. He could see the stove from his bed and the bathroom from the stove. It had enough room to have a guest over, but he spent most of his time alone. He did not mind being alone. It was very comfortable for him, and he liked being in the space when he was the only one there. It made him feel strong, like he was a young man again.

From the window, he could see the trees. When he first moved into the apartment, the trees were barely visible. At the time, they were, much like him, in the spring of their youth. He could never have imagined they would grow so strong and tall so that he could look out the window and see their great branches flourishing. In the summer, the trees helped keep the apartment cool, and he liked to look at them from the window.

The jagged coastline sat just beyond the trees, and the man was just close enough to smell the sea. He liked to stand at the window and smell the sea. He stood at the window and imagined thousands of fish swimming all night while he slept, discovering while he dreamt. He liked to think of the fish at night, swimming while the world went dark. It made him very happy to think of the fish, and he went to the window every night to think of the fish before he went to sleep. Sometimes he had trouble sleeping, and it helped him to think of the fish. He made sure that they were the last thing he thought about each night.

When the morning arrived, his alarm went off at just the time the sun was beginning to rise. The man would walk from his bed to the window. He thought of the fish and wondered where they had traveled while he slept. Had they discovered a sunken treasure? Swam to greater depths than ever before? Did they reunite with old family members? Were they caught in the merciless gaze of a shark? He didn't like to think of this, and he would quickly dismiss the possibility. The fish had swum unharmed while he slept. They had swum gloriously, in and out of coral coves, ducking further below the surface. They were illuminated with colors, swimming majestically below an open sky, their gills flapping as they reached their destination safely, over and over.

After concluding the fish were as they should be, he walked to the kitchen and made a fresh cup of coffee and a cup of tea. He took both cups to the table and drank the coffee. He drank the coffee as slow as he could without allowing it to get cold. He could remember when he didn't like coffee in the morning. But now he liked it. He liked it very much, and he poured a cup every morning. He sat in the same seat at the table, and he drank it while it stayed hot. He drank it with the sun coming up and the cup of tea nearby. When he sat down, he removed the tea bag even before taking his first sip of coffee. He pulled the string carefully, lifted the bag, and placed it in the saucer. As he drank his cup of coffee, he watched the steam rise from the cup of tea. The steam rose much like the sun, while the man sat quietly, and the fish rested after a long night of swimming while the man slept.

Once he finished his cup of coffee, he would set it next to the sink alongside the cup of tea. He grabbed a croissant and a bottle of water and walked out of his apartment. He turned right on the steep road and walked up toward the top of the hill. He used to walk the hill without breathing heavily, but now he gulped the air and was out of breath by the time he reached the top. He liked the feeling of breathing hard in the morning, and he thought of the fish who swam so effortlessly through the night while he slept. He thought of their nighttime adventures and how they continually avoided the gaze of the great sharks. At the top of the road, he walked out onto the trail. He felt the sun warming as it rose steadily, while the wind cooled his cheeks as he stood atop the cliffs. It was an invigorating feeling to have risen with the sun and now stand on top of the cliffs. By now, the sun had risen higher than he could ever climb, but each of them had risen for another day together and climbed while the fish slept. On top of the cliffs, he would always turn toward the water and let the sun warm his back. He gazed out over the Atlantic and wondered where the fish had journeyed to the night before. Did they wait for the sun to rise like he did? No. Of course not, he thought. They were waiting for the boats and fishermen to disappear, the kayaks to go home, and the sun to set. They were waiting for the world to go dark, for the old man to stand by the window before bed, so they could swim all night while he dreamed.

The man walked south, meandering along the trail. There was a lighthouse at the point. Once he got to the lighthouse, he would rest. He would rest when he got there. He would sit on the rocks and rest, but he didn't rush getting there. He was not in a hurry. The sun was barely in the sky, and there was no reason to rush. The wind was nice and cool and the sun on his back was warm. The waves were gentle, and the beach was perfect down below as he looked out over the water. He made sure not to get too close to the edge without rails, and he thought of the fish that could never fall so long as they remained in the sea.

His family used to take this walk together. They would wake up in their small flat and set out for the majestic cliffs. The three of them would walk up the steep road with ease and head toward the lighthouse. They would hold hands and stare at the ocean with the sun at their backs and the cool air blowing their hair while the sun rose higher than they could climb.

He would never forget the impulse. He loved her, and he had turned to her and embraced her for what only seemed like a second. He was not a spontaneous man, but the moment had inspired him. He had wanted to squeeze her tight that morning, and so he did so without contemplating the gesture.

The couple had only lost sight of their son for a second. Less than a second it seemed. It couldn't have been longer than two. But the small boy had walked too close to the edge with no railing and his tiny body had vanished forever by the time they separated from their embrace.

On that morning, all the fish in the sea heard their cries when they looked over the edge toward the rocks with green moss and the sand without a single footprint. The fish swam out to sea, as far as they could, away from the terrible cries on the shore. They swam as if they had been found in the gaze of the great shark with the sun overhead, the lighthouse in the distance, the rocks topped with bright emerald moss, and the cliffs lined all along the shore.

# A GOOD LISTENER

ndre was young. He was in his late twenties. Small. About five foot, seven inches and very unimposing. He had olive skin and he moved around the bar area with surprising calm. In fact, he never hurried. There was nothing hurried about him. He moved calmly and methodically behind the bar, and this never changed. Truth be told, he moved as if life would have to travel at his pace.

André had worked at the bar since he was a teenager. He started out cleaning toilets and sweeping the floors. He didn't like the work, but he liked doing it well. The bar had been here on the southwest coast of Portugal for many years. In fact, one of his earliest memories was coming here with his dad to watch Portugal play a match in the World Cup. He had never forgotten the look of joy on his father's face when they defeated England on penalties to earn a place in the semi-final. A massive roar went up among the patrons in the bar, and André noticed the bartender cut a demure, wry smile. He smiled calmly as he cleared empty glasses while the people celebrated. Nobody else even noticed the bartender, but André liked the fact that he did.

Whether the bar was crowded or empty, André approached his job the same way. He was wholly unaffected by the number of customers, as it made no difference to him. He made all the same gestures, navigating the area behind the bar with the certainty of a man many years his senior. He moved like a man who knew about life, its struggles, and his role in people's lives. He was a young man of real perspective and this could be deducted by watching him work.

He performed every task behind the bar at precisely the same pace—turning to the side to collect a tip, reaching for a new glass, or finishing the garnishing. His style wasn't so much robotic as professional. There was a natural quality to all the procedural labors of bartending, and he could even make sweeping the floor look like a fluid, graceful art.

The bar itself was spotless. You could almost see yourself in the sheen of the multi-colored marble. The stemware he set down had been cleaned without so much as a spot visible. Every inch of the bar was immaculate, and André insisted on this condition. He insisted on it, and it was not negotiable. He was a perfectionist, and there was no situation that could precipitate a compromise in his approach.

André refused to let the customers influence his approach either. If people needed to wait a bit longer, so be it. If they got up and chose to leave, that was their choice. He never felt even a touch of guilt. This was his office, his domain after all, and he would never make adjustments in order to serve more customers or serve customers more quickly. This he could not do, would not do. He moved to his own rhythms, like the sun or the moon, the warm breeze blowing outside the window or the tides of the sea.

In a sense, he accomplished what few ever do. He controlled time. Time existed on his terms, not the other way around. He set the pace, and it was beautiful— measured, patient, and elegant. He never came unhinged, and his patrons either had to embrace his calm, elegant whims or grow frustrated with them. It was their choice.

At the end of the night, André never rushed people out, and there was always enough time to pour another drink.

However, the bar was his first priority, and the bar came before the people who frequented it. If there was one customer whose needs were always met, it was the actual bar itself, and this was visible in every perfect leather barstool or high-top table or exquisite drink that provided an accurate reflection of the bartender's eternal devotion to his establishment.

When someone walked in and took a seat at the bar, André would often greet them and then proceed to wipe the bar or return a utensil to its proper place while the customer waited to order their drink. This could be off-putting, but he did so without apology.

He would offer a polite hello, but he wasn't the type of bartender you cozied up to. He was closer to an artist than a friend. There was a slight social awkwardness about him, and he didn't emanate a natural warmth that simply made people feel better. He didn't pride himself in the art of conversation, witty quips, or a slap on the back among pals. He was more focused on his craft, and if you had come looking for a piece of advice or a shoulder to cry on, he likely wasn't your man.

However, André was a good listener. If there was one thing about being less talkative, it's that you always have the opportunity to listen. You have the chance to absorb, if not respond, and he did. People unloaded their problems while they waited for his drinks. They told him about their troubles at the office, friends they had lost, and hollow marriages. These matters of the heart were not his specialty, but he understood that people needed to talk to someone and that they enjoyed the sound of their own voices more than anyone else's. People drinking alcohol enjoyed the sound of their own voices most of all. Although he was no conversationalist, he was smart enough to understand that people needed feedback. It was only human nature for people to crave validation in some form. And he offered this in the way of a steady gaze, an understanding face, and eyes void of judgment.

So, they talked. They talked and talked and talked—over gin and tonics, scotch, cervezas, wine, and every drink imaginable. They talked from the moment they sat down at the bar until he shut it down for the night. They talked with the coastal breeze blowing in and the sound of the sea just beyond the door. They talked while he fixed drinks perfectly, with exotic creativity, and while he wiped the bar clean. Their voices ran continuously through his head, never seeping in too deep, more like a soundtrack, a kaleidoscope of elevator music that provided the background music for his natural rhythmic movements around the bar.

Tomas was a regular at the bar. He had been for years. He was a local businessman, and he liked the mixture of locals and tourists that the bar attracted. He would never have been considered an alcoholic, but he appreciated a good drink. A stiff drink. His preference was a gin and tonic, and André made the best gin and tonics he had ever tasted. They were different. Fresher. Brighter. Somehow just a bit more cared for. There really was no comparison, and he always looked forward to stopping at the bar near the end of the day and enjoying a gin and tonic on his way home.

Tomas was in his early fifties—young enough to still look ahead but not without recognizing he had created more memories in the past than he would in the future. He was on the back nine now to be sure, and he could feel it. He was a successful businessman. Worked in finance, André had heard. Divorced. No kids. A plethora of pals it seemed. But he always came to the bar alone. This was his place, and he never had company here. He liked to drink alone and enjoy his gin and tonic sitting at the bar with the sea at his back.

Even though time had begun to erode his appearance, Tomas was still handsome. In his youth, he might have been really good looking, the kind of guy who might have turned heads the moment he walked in the room. But the years had taken some of his hair and put a bit of weight on his once athletic frame. Still, Tomas possessed a certain charisma, and he would often attract the interest of single ladies at the bar. Tomas politely refused these advances, and he would talk to André while he sat the bar with his gin and tonic.

Tomas liked to watch André make his gin and tonics. It was a long, perfect process. André would begin with the fruit, carving gorgeous mangoes and strawberries and raspberries, wiping the blade of the knife each time he made an incision. The fruit lay in front of the bartender in perfect order, lined and cut to perfection. So much so that it almost seemed unfortunate to hand these colorful pieces over to the gin and tonic. But they were both an intricate part of the presentation and the product. They surrounded the black straw, encompassed the cubes of ice, and permeated the liquid (alongside a few other mysterious ingredients) inside the large bulbous glasses that André used. It was all very decadent and, combined with gin and tonic water, offered an exciting and refreshing experience. Tomas could always count on André's gin and tonics at the end of a long day. They never failed him once.

"André, have you ever seen the movie *Three Days of the Condor*?" asked Tomas. André shook his head no. "You remind me of the assassin Joubert when he tells Robert Redford's character that 'There is no cause. There is only yourself. And the belief is in your precision.' That's you, André. God dammit, that's you! I envy men like you."

André chuckled, shaking his head from side to side. Tomas was too much, but that was one of the things André liked about him.

Tomas wasn't normally this loud, but he was often entertaining. He frequently arrived with a story to tell, but there never seemed to be any bullshit in his tales. And he never seemed to sugarcoat them. On this night, he sipped his drink slowly. Slower than normal. Letting the delicious drink stay in his mouth for a moment. Tasting all the flavor. Savoring it.

When André moved closer in order to sweep away the straw on the counter, Tomas said plainly, "I am going to kill myself tonight."

André stopped for a moment, looked at Tomas in the face, and removed the straw from the counter. He turned slightly to his right and discarded it into the wastebasket. As per usual, he didn't say anything, but he kept his eyes focused on Tomas.

"It's time to get on with it," said Tomas. "There really is no reason to put it off."

André nodded, not disapprovingly, and moved to the other side of the bar where a couple had sat down together.

Most couples didn't sit at the bar. At least not older couples who had been married for many years. They usually requested a quiet table with a little more refinery and pomp or a more comfortable seat. He didn't know why, but he always liked it when he saw an old, married couple take up a couple of barstools.

André always liked a bar. It was different, and he remembered when his dad would take him out to watch those *fútbol* matches here. Sitting at the bar made him feel special in a way that sitting at a table did not, and he wondered if other people felt the same way. Perhaps it was because you sat up higher. He wasn't sure, but he liked the feeling of sitting at a bar from the first moment. He liked sitting at it, and he liked working behind it.

A bar is different, André thought. It beckons you …
and requires that you approach it. When the drinks are
poured and the food is served, you have to lean forward
just a touch, rest your arms on the granite, and sit with
your back to the room. It takes courage to sit with your
back to the room, André thought. Real cojones. You
couldn't be insecure or concerned about your image.
Couples often seemed to lack this quality.

"*Rioja*," said the woman. "Not your best. Not your
worst."

"Gin and tonic for me," said the man.

André nodded and began to prepare their drinks
behind the bar. He liked that the woman had ordered her
own drink. Men often felt the need to order drinks for
their dates, but André could see the woman preferred to
order her own drink. Of course, her husband knew this
too.

The husband and wife sat at the bar. He placed his
right hand atop her left, which she had placed on the bar.
He smiled at her, and she leaned her head against his
shoulder. They didn't say a word to one another, sitting
with their backs to the room, to the nonsense of so many
stilted conversations and false pretenses. They never

turned around. They aren't here to be seen, André thought. He felt a quiet admiration for them as he brought them their drinks. He wasn't married, but he hoped he would be someday. He hoped he could find a wife who would sit at a bar, without the need to make incessant small talk, who would lean against his shoulder and was unafraid to keep the world at bay.

André moved back toward the other side of the bar. He began polishing glasses in front of Tomas.

"This gin and tonic is effing good," said Tomas. "You outdid yourself, André. Damn good. Some things never get old."

André cracked a smile without teeth.

"Tonight's the night André. Going to blow my fucking brains out. Going to end the misery and suffering. Put a big fat conclusion on it. Told my ex-wife. Mentioned it to a couple of buddies. They did all they could to talk me out of it. They told me I was selfish. They told me I would never do it. Threw every guilt trip at me they could think of, but it's been a long time coming."

André kept polishing the glasses, listening, his head slightly bowed. He had a special soap that got the glasses clean and he liked to polish them to make sure there were no imperfections. He liked to polish them when he listened. And he always liked to listen to Tomas. He always gave it to André straight and asked for little. He never sought pity or comfort, but he liked to talk, and he wasn't afraid to lay it on the line. André liked that about him. He seemed less full of shit than most of the people who came to the bar, who talked just to hear themselves talk or garner praise for their infantile gloating and boasting. Tomas wasn't like that.

The older couple at the bar ordered another round. They had lived a long time, André thought. They had lived a long time and lived through a lot of pain, he thought. Their faces had deep lines and, while he could see the wile in their eyes when they smiled, there was a lot of life lived behind those eyes. Hard life. Real life. Tragedies that had arrived unforeseen. The kind of losses you can't come back from, that leave people broken and can never make them whole again. The kind that keep people fighting for one another to the end, he thought, as he watched the man continuing to caress her hand. Everyone needs someone to fight for them, he thought.

The man and the woman finished their drinks, paid for them, and left André a generous tip before they slipped out the door without saying goodbye.

"You know what pisses me off the most about my ex-wife?" Tomas asked without waiting for an answer since he was going to answer the question himself. "I don't even think she cares if I go through with it or not. She might even want me to if it weren't for the burden of guilt. She just doesn't want to have to live with the idea that I took my own life after all the fucked-up things she's done to me. She just doesn't want it on her conscience. Can you believe that shit? Now that's fucked up. All about her. It's always been all about her."

André listened closely. He had stopped polishing the glasses. Now that the old couple had left the bar, Tomas was the only one there. He was sitting where he always sat, with the bar glistening underneath the lights and his arms on the granite countertop. André had stopped working altogether and was looking Tomas in the eyes, trying to hear every word he said without reacting to them.

When Tomas was done with his drink, he stood up and slapped his right hand on the top of the bar. André waved him off when Tomas tried to reach for his wallet, looked at him with his knowing eyes, and respectfully extended his right hand.

André went home and went to bed. He couldn't stop thinking about Tomas. When he woke the next morning, he was still thinking about him. André wondered whether Tomas had actually gone through with it, and he had a sense of dread that made him feel pretty certain that he had.

In the morning, André made a fresh cup of coffee, grabbed a muffin, and sat down to read the newspaper. He went about his day as he always did, and he hoped his instincts were wrong about the seriousness of Tomas' intentions. But he trusted his instincts, and they were rarely wrong.

When André arrived at work that night, he was still thinking of Tomas. André took off his jacket and hung it up in the back before returning to get the bar prepared for the evening. When he looked down, he noticed that a thin, white envelope was sitting underneath the bar next to a row of high ball glasses. André wasn't sure how it had gotten there, but he opened it with cautious curiosity. There was a note inside. The note read:

To the bartender who makes drinks so spectacular, they could cure the ills of the world, the man who said so little and meant so much, who let me leave this world on my own terms and did what no one else could—the man who fought for me by not putting up a fight.

*– Tomas*

André read the letter over and over, retracing the words. André was a man who lived life on his own terms. He read the note once more and thought about Tomas. He thought of the old couple, the lines on their faces, and the weight of time. He thought of the great distances, the vastness of the ocean, and all the miles to travel. He thought of Tomas and his stories and the gin and tonics he had ordered over all the years. André thought of Tomas as the sun began to sink. He reached for a glass and began polishing it. People would be there soon.

# THE GIRL AT THE CHOCOLATE SHOP

E ach morning, it was one of the first stores to open in Granada. Most stores in Granada didn't open early. If it was dark out, stores were closed. They opened as the sun rose.

The Chocolate Shop was different. It didn't seem to be affected by neighborhood trends, and it opened while it was still dark outside. It was a small space, tucked on a corner, and it had large glass doors on each side that allowed you to enter from either of the converging streets. If the doors were open just a crack, you could smell the aroma of fresh bread seeping into the streets. When the lights went on in the shop, with the sky still dark and the world still quiet, the shop gleamed a warm glow.

The Chocolate Shop was nothing if not inviting. It didn't just serve chocolate. It served bread, much of which was covered in chocolate or filled with chocolate or dipped in chocolate. Donuts with frosting. Neapolitans. You could find just about any sweet treat, just sitting there displayed in the glass case, inside the shop with the glass windows, while the sky was still dark.

This made The Chocolate Shop a perfect place for people to begin the day, and all different types of people would stop in each morning on their way to somewhere else. Government officials. Lawyers. College students. Parents, stumbling in still tired, after dropping their children off at school.

The shop was tiny. It offered barely enough space for people to stand while waiting to place their order and, if there were more than three people in line, they were forced to wait outside until there was enough space to stand inside the shop. But it was worth it. Warm bread and chocolate were worth it, especially on a colder day with a little nip in the air, when no other place was open, and the sky was still dark.

The girl who worked at The Chocolate Shop had long blond hair. She was, in truth, a young woman, but she could easily have passed for sixteen or seventeen years of age. Each morning, she arrived at the shop in the dark, before any of the customers, and made sure that the food was warm and fresh and good. There is nothing like fresh bread in the morning, but it requires work in the dark in order for it to arrive fresh for customers at the beginning of the day.

The girl was always punctual, and customers appreciated that the shop opened on time. It opened every day, and she was never late. This was very rare in Spain. In fact, very few shops are open every day and even fewer open on time. But it was always open, and she was always on time. The Chocolate Shop was an exception.

The girl at The Chocolate Shop went about her job with perfectly acceptable certainty. She listened as the customers spoke, put their orders together, and calculated the amount of money they owed. She was good at math, and she did these calculations in her head. She had always been good at math, and this was easy for her. She did these calculations each morning, with the sky still dark and people on their way to begin their day. She did this with competence, and she smiled not only politely but warmly. It was true she smiled the way employees were required to smile at customers, but there was a personal quality to her smile. This is to say that she smiled from the inside rather than the outside. They are not the same thing. To smile from the inside is different. And she always smiled from the inside. In all the time she had worked there, she had never smiled in what might have been construed as a cursory, inauthentic manner.

There were all kinds of theories as to why she offered more with her smile, but it was only speculation. And gossip never really leads to the truth. It only serves to make people feel better, like they can somehow understand a behavior so long as they can surmise the root of its origin. Was she just flirting? Some people said she was on the run. Others said she was just in it for tips. Some even wondered if she was using the store as a front to deal narcotics while projecting herself as the most friendly, normal, unsuspecting person alive. Mind you, not a single one of these theories was rooted in an ounce of truth. And so she simply showed up each day, flexing the corners of her mouth in a manner that conveyed much but revealed little until one day she didn't.

When she first started the job at The Chocolate Shop, she was happy. She may not have made clear the reason for her happiness, but it was true. She was truly happy. In those early days, she communicated this with a buoyant, hopeful affect, and she never appeared bitter or impatient or worn down—like she eventually did over time. In her final months at the shop, she had become downright sullen, almost ornery to the point where it was something a customer had to consider before entering the store. It wasn't good for business, but The Chocolate Shop had an advantage on the competition, since other establishments didn't open nearly as early. The Chocolate Shop was filled with delicious treats, was the only place open, and customers were willing to endure her now relatively unpleasant demeanor.

She would never forget the day she told him, the anxiety and excitement she felt all at once. She was still young. She had started working at The Chocolate Shop after finishing secondary school a couple of years before. José was a year older and had just begun his third year studying business at the University of Granada. He also worked part time in a clothing store in the city center. He was very handsome, with dark skin, dark eyes, and impeccably styled hair. But he was also solid. His character was solid, unflinching. His eyes never drifted when he spoke, and he had a quality about his person that always illustrated he could be trusted.

They had moved in together once she finished *Bachillerato*, and they were managing to pay their bills. The apartment was in a neighborhood where lots of university students lived near Plaza Los Lobos and not far from the Lemon Rock Hostel where they liked to hang out and listen to music in the evenings from time to time. They rented an ordinary flat. It was a tiny one-bedroom, but it was theirs. It was theirs, and they lived there with thoughts and dreams and hopes of what the future held, and what their life together might become in the years ahead.

Spain, even in the modern era, was still not terribly modern. It remained predominantly Catholic, and their parents, especially her parents, didn't approve of their living situation. But they were adults. They asked next to nothing from their parents and received even less. They were essentially on their own, but part of them liked it that way. It made them feel strong, and it gave them confidence that they could face the future together and come out ahead.

She was trying to figure out the best time to tell him. It wasn't an easy thing to say, and she decided to tell him on a Saturday morning when they both had the day off. This way they could be free of any distractions or competing responsibilities. She would have his full attention, which wasn't always easy to obtain with school and work intruding on their lives.

They woke in the morning, with a sliver of light slashing through the window down the slender corridor between apartment buildings. She brushed her teeth, put on a nice pair of jeans, a cream shirt with buttons, and some stylish leather boots. From their small apartment, they walked to their favorite breakfast restaurant, Baraka, between the cathedral and the Monastery.

Baraka was a small place with both indoor and outdoor seating and incredible baked scrambled eggs that arrived in piping hot, white dishes. Scrambled eggs in Spain are not uncommon, but they were rarely baked, and at Baraka they were exquisite. They were hot and fresh and quite unique, and they provided the perfect complement to an array of breads, fruits, and juices that Baraka served as well. It was a lovely place.

"You look nice, Sofía," said José.

"I'm pregnant," said Sofía.

José just sat there stunned. He wasn't expecting this news. He knew they were careful, and he wasn't ready to be a parent. He loved Sofía, but that did little to change his feelings. They were young, after all. He liked their freedom, to go to the Lemon Rock and listen to music on Friday night or head out with friends or drive to Salobreña for the day. Still, he tried not to respond in a manner that illustrated all of the things that were rushing through his head.

"I, I don't know what to say," he offered, uneasily. This clearly wasn't the worst response he could have delivered, but it was hardly a joyous one either. But José was smart. For all his youth and inexperience, he was smart, and he knew this was a time when it was better to let Sofía talk than add much of his own narrative to the conversation.

"I know we aren't ready for this," she went on. "I am not trying to kid myself. But I also know that my first response wasn't anger or frustration or disappointment. It was hope and excitement that I was carrying your child, our child. Nothing about the situation felt unwanted or undesirable. Unexpected, yes, but not undesirable. It felt fortunate. I felt fortunate. I love you, after all. I love you, José, and I have always dreamed of having children, having your children, having our children. But I know. We are young. We are barely making ends meet and you are in school. I work at a chocolate shop and leave early each morning. And we aren't married, and this is Spain. I know. I know. I know. That this would fly in the face of everything we've planned, that it would stunt a hundred other dreams we want to come true. I know. I know. God damn. I know."

She was emotional. People in Spain don't say "God damn" or "Jesus" unless they are emotional. And, even then, they try not too … at all costs.

José was steady, and he let her talk. He let her talk and think aloud and talk some more without saying a word. She told him just how she was feeling, and she let him know that a myriad of emotions were coursing through her. The pendulum swung back and forth, and she seemed to be talking faster the less he offered. It was slightly awkward, and he sensed he might be about to break down.

"But, Sof—" he began.

She cut him off. "Don't even say it, José," she interjected. "Don't even fucking say it."

"I love you, too, Sof," he said gently now. "I do. I always have. I just think. I just … I am just not sure we are ready."

"Sometimes that's how it is, José," said Sofía. "Sometimes in life you aren't ready, and you just have to find a way to be or learn to be or make up your mind to be. Sorry if this isn't convenient for you."

"Sof, come on," he said. "That's not fair. I didn't say it was inconvenient."

"You didn't have to," said Sofía. "It's all over your face. You don't want this. At least not right now. You don't want to have this baby with me."

"It's not that I don't want to," said José. "I am just not sure we should. They aren't the same thing. There are times wanting something isn't enough to make it a good decision."

Sofía didn't say anything for quite some time. She just sat there in the restaurant, which had now filled up, and she looked around the room at the other couples and families and a few people eating alone. She wondered about their lives, the decisions they had made, the choices they had been faced with, the choices that hadn't been easy.

The woman at the table next to her was alone. Was she alone because she too had been faced with a decision of great consequence? Did one choice many years ago instruct all that was to follow? Do the dominoes fall just like that? Would it be the same for her?

She looked down at her eggs and took a bite. Even in the middle of such an intense conversation, she was hungry, and the eggs tasted good. They were good, and her appetite only seemed to increase following the dialogue. José ate less. He sipped his freshly squeezed orange juice and politely asked for another coffee. And he took out a cigarette and lit it since they were seated outside. He didn't smoke often, especially not early in the day, but the moment seemed to call for it. He inhaled the smoke and stared at the people passing by the restaurant, perhaps heading toward the Monastery of San Jerónimo, which was close by. It was a beautiful monastery with a lovely courtyard and a magnificent, ornate altar.

"What will your parents think, Sof?" asked José.

"My parents. My parents. Really? My effing parents! We've been together for over three years, and you've never once cared, really cared, what they thought of anything. Now, all of a sudden, they are of great concern to you because you know they will be pissed. Fuck you, José."

He knew he had said the wrong thing. He knew it the minute he said it. And he also knew her parents would want them to keep the baby and get married as soon as possible. But he knew they wouldn't make life easier, and he had chosen to remind Sofía of something that needed no reminding. José was realizing the less he said the better. He needed to rely on his steadiness rather than say anything that could be considered contentious. Even reasonable questions had no place in this conversation.

"Well, I want to have the baby, José," Sofía declared emphatically. "I want to have this baby, and that is exactly what I plan to do. If you don't like it, I don't care. That's right, José. I don't care. I don't fucking care."

Sofía knew this was a risky tactic, that she ran the possibility of alienating José, of losing him for good, of ending up alone with her baby or in a loveless marriage where the resentment would hang over it like a scrim of sound for all eternity. But she said it anyway, and José listened. He listened, as he pulled another drag on his cigarette and he ate the best eggs in Granada. Neither of them said another word for a long time until José signaled to the waitress and requested the check. "*La cuenta, por favor*," he said with an uneasy, earnest smile.

The waitress had kept her distance, realizing the two of them were in the middle of a serious conversation. But now she brought the check over as requested. José paid the bill and left a bit larger tip than was normally the custom in Spain. He grabbed Sofía's shoulder bag and handed it to her and then he grabbed her hand. He grabbed her hand tenderly, his fingers entwined with hers, and she squeezed it back. They walked out of the restaurant a young couple, a different couple, with the Granada sunlight now beginning to rain down and the upper reaches of the tower of the great cathedral now visible overhead as they strolled past the fruit stands in Plaza Romanilla.

In the days that followed, they told no one. José went to school and worked in the clothing store. And Sofía went to The Chocolate Shop, just as she had done the day before and the day before that. She went to The Chocolate Shop, and she didn't smile.

José tried to be more understanding of Sofía's wishes, and he also made an effort to be more patient, loving, and careful about what he said. She felt his compassion. This didn't change what Sofía knew to be true regarding José's opinion, but it helped. Just a little. It helped to feel that he was there, that he was there for her, just for her, and that he would be there.

This went on for a couple of weeks, the two of them taking a bit of extra care with one another and saying nothing of Sofía's pregnancy. This allowed them to return to their lives, their daily lives, in ways they would never be able to once the baby was born. Most of all, the time allowed them to distance themselves from the raw, unbridled emotions that ran through each of them the moment they learned the news. Sofía was able to take a step back and think more objectively, and José was able to do the same.

José learned a lot in those weeks. He knew that what mattered most to him was Sofía. He still didn't believe they were ready to be parents, but he wasn't going anywhere. He would be there for her, and he would respect her decision. Not just respect it but embrace it. Love it. He would love her decision because he loved her, and he fully expected to become the best husband and father he could be. Sofía saw José trying. She saw him taking on extra shifts at work and asking how she was feeling and doing all the little things responsible parents have to do, and it broke her heart. It broke her heart to see the manner in which he was responding, and she now knew, if there had ever been any doubt, that he loved her very much.

When Sofía made the decision to terminate the pregnancy, José went with her to the doctor. They didn't tell their families. They didn't inform their friends or coworkers or classmates. Only the two of them knew and they discussed it only with God and asked for his forgiveness along with one another's. The procedure itself was less than Sofía had expected. The doctor was competent and helped her relax and it went well. But the weight of her decision was greater than she could ever have imagined. How could a decision made on the wings of reason and logic feel so awful? How could the guilt be so overwhelming? How could it all feel so vile and troubling and terribly wrong? And how could she live out the rest of her days knowing, not merely what she had done, but how she felt—guilty and hollow and ashamed? Moreover, it was all so final, so unimaginably final.

José was there to support Sofía through her grief but, truth be told, he himself was relieved. He felt slightly guilty to feel this way, but the guilt faded with time, and the relief returned the color to his face. His life was before him once again, and he could see the future, weightless and full of possibility. There was some disappointment that he wouldn't be a father now, and he felt the pangs of this at some level. But there was still time for them, and these laments didn't compare to the relieved feeling of hitting the reset button and being able to return to the way things were. Each day it got just a bit easier, and he could imagine a time in the not so distant future when he no longer thought about the pregnancy or about Sofía's difficult decision to terminate it.

For Sofía, there was no such sense of relief. No refuge. There were no peaceful evenings, no bright days at The Chocolate Shop, and she couldn't ever imagine that she would smile, really smile, from the inside, ever again. There was a sense that if she did, it would have almost been inauthentic, and so she went to work every day laced with a comatose sadness. She arrived early, prepared the bread, organized the shop, and never smiled. Customers came and went and wondered about her sour appearance. She said nothing, and she never smiled. She never smiled at the people who entered the shop. She wouldn't smile, couldn't, it seemed. Not really. Not after having made the decision she made. It was a decision made thoughtfully, but it was made entirely with her cognitive abilities. Her heart told her something different. Her heart wanted to keep the baby, and now it was broken. Her heart was broken, and she couldn't smile. She wouldn't smile, not from the inside. She would never smile from the inside, way down deep, the way she once did, ever again.

One morning in the spring, months later, José left the apartment and walked toward school. Sofía walked in the opposite direction, toward The Chocolate Shop, only this time she just kept walking, past the glass windows, with the doors still locked, the lights out, people waiting outside, and nobody inside to warm the bread. The windowpanes were large and dark and facing the street. Sofía didn't even so much as turn her head. It was now springtime, and the leaves were once again fastening themselves to the trees. Springtime in Granada. The morning air was fresh and there was now only a faint glimpse of snow that remained, dusted splendidly across the tops of the Sierra Nevada mountains.

Around the corner from The Chocolate Shop, Sofía stopped to look at her face in the reflection of a window. It was the window of a bank that wouldn't open for hours. She gazed into the glass pane, past her golden hair and perfect skin and into the dullness of her eyes. She wondered if she would have looked different had she decided to keep the baby. Would the mirror have reflected another image? She could never be sure, but she wondered. She wondered, and she thought about how her life would be different and whether or not she would have still looked so very young and felt so frighteningly old.

# MONTADITOS IN CÁDIZ

It was late when we arrived in Cádiz. It was late and the air was dark. Dark and cool with a low fog moving in across the bay. We crossed a long bridge and then our car was deposited onto the small peninsula hanging off the southwestern edge of Spain. As we threaded our vehicle through the narrow corridors of the old city, people crossed carelessly in front of us while children played in the generous, flat plaza. Eventually, we found an underground garage, parked our car, grabbed our bags out of the trunk, and traveled the rest of the way to our hotel on foot.

The hotel was converted from an old family home in the center of town. We entered through a massive wooden door to find ourselves standing in a giant stone lobby with a ceiling that appeared as if it was ten floors up. It was actually more like a giant atrium, and there were plants and trees to give the space a more natural feeling. The space was dark with only a few lights on the wall. It was dark and brooding and dramatic, much like the city itself.

Cádiz is a magnificent old city in Andalucía, perched on the precipice of Europe. It is one of the oldest continually inhabited places on earth, and they have been importing plants to soften the hard edifices and architectural lines for years. In fact, Columbus brought dozens of palm trees back to Cádiz from the New World, and they stand to this day as something of an oasis in the green spaces within the city. Most people don't even know that Columbus sailed to the New World from Cádiz—on both his second voyage in 1493 and his fourth in 1502. Largely forgotten in the modern world, Cádiz was relevant for centuries, home to the Phoenicians and Romans and once an epicenter of trade, exploration, and imperial might.

Inside the hotel, we got the keys from the woman at the small desk downstairs and made our way to our room. Keys. Yes, keys. This old building still used keys, and it was nice to feel the long silver key with teeth and definition, weighty in the palm of my hand, instead of the generic plastic cards used by hotels these days. The doors to the rooms were also heavy and old, and there was something substantial about placing the key in the door and turning the lock to enter our room, entering, late at night, up the stairs, in this ancient city. It was like being in an old castle, and it felt as if we should have been carrying lanterns.

After my family got settled and the kids went to sleep, I headed out to walk around the city a bit and pick up a few items for breakfast the next day. It was Saturday night, and the dark shadows of evening had descended. The shops had closed. There were still some convenience stores open and there were bars and restaurants with a few chairs spilled out into the narrow streets.

The streets in Cádiz were not well lit. They were narrow and dark and there was an ominous, incandescent aura that hung like a cloak over the city. Perhaps ominous isn't precisely the right word, but Cádiz felt more rugged, worn, and unshaven than other historic cities in Andalucía. The streets weren't quite as clean and tidy. The people walked with slightly heavier feet. And it seemed to get dark earlier in the day. You felt the city's endurance and the raw, survival instincts that had allowed it to sustain itself across so many centuries.

As I walked from our hotel down a long, quiet street, I was surprised there weren't more places open, particularly places to eat. Spaniards routinely eat in the middle of the night, and it was still relatively early for Spain. However, a number of establishments were closed and, for a moment, I wasn't sure I would find anything until morning. It was a disappointment to think I might not get something to eat, since I was hungry.

In Spain, it doesn't really matter what hours are on the door or what the Internet says. Places open when they open and call it a day when it suits them. As the sign on one restaurant said: "We are open unless we are closed." This is a foreign concept to Americans, and there was something both inspiring and frustrating about this philosophy Spaniards embraced. Either way, you can either be frustrated or flexible, and so I continued to walk down the ancient corridors, plunging myself deeper into the city and the night. It almost felt as if I was traveling back in time, but I liked it. I liked the darkness and the rough buildings and the solitude that filled the space and the night. It made me feel as if I could be swallowed whole at any moment, and it made my other preoccupations seem small. I liked feeling small and invisible, not standing out, and quietly becoming part of the fabric.

We had traveled a pretty fair distance during the day and, more than anything, I was ready to eat. So, I just kept walking. The architecture was beautiful, and it is hard to be anything but fully present in Cádiz, feeling the weight of so much history captured in the city's long, steely gaze. It is quietly imposing. It stalks you, almost overwhelms you, and I enjoyed feeling the long lope of centuries seep in.

I had nearly given up on getting something to eat when I spotted a light up ahead on the right. I could see there were a couple of people smoking cigarettes in the street outside the small restaurant, and I stepped inside hoping they were still serving food. The tiny restaurant was sunken, requiring me to step down as I entered from street level. Inside, the floor was checkerboard black and white, and there was a nice wooden bar and a few small tables arranged informally within the small space.

I felt a sigh of relief when the man behind the counter assured me they were still serving food and handed me a menu with dozens of *montaditos* filled with everything from squid to eggs. Even before I entered, I could smell the scent of fresh bread wafting into the street, and so the vast array of choices was a welcome sight to my palate and my hunger. The aroma was tantalizing, and it seemed fitting that such an unassuming place might indeed be the gateway to what smelled like the food of the gods.

I sat down on a plain, black barstool and looked over the menu. There were a couple of women sitting at a table having a drink, but the rest of the place was empty—save for the man behind the bar and the man cooking in the kitchen who I could see through the rectangular picture window. Even so, I felt slightly underdressed or perhaps just dressed poorly compared to the standards set by people in Spain—who always take the time to put themselves together. They comb their hair, shave their faces, and select shirts with collars when going out to a restaurant. They wear shoes with at least a hint of style, and they wouldn't be caught dead in athletic clothes unless they were exercising. These are hardly high standards, but they are standards. More importantly, they are embraced by the entire population.

"*De donde eres?*" said the man behind the bar.

"Los Angeles," I said.

He looked at me suspiciously, not necessarily impressed, but interested enough.

"My name's Victor," he said. "From Cádiz. Lived here my whole life."

Victor was in his early fifties. He had a thick head of hair, a small belly, and that olive complexion that so many Spaniards possess. He had dark eyes that were somehow both warm and rough, and he found a way to be welcoming in a manner that was aggressive but not personal.

"*Para comer?*" he said.

"*Si,*" I responded, almost nervously.

"The *montaditos* are very good," he said. "The best in Cádiz."

Cádiz wasn't known for its cuisine so much as its beverages, with nearly all of the sherry on earth produced in this region. Much like port originating from Porto, sherry comes from a triangle of cities here in this corner of the province, and the production of wine in Cádiz dates back to Roman times, before the Moors ruled Spain. But Victor swore I would not be disappointed by the *montaditos.*

The *montadito* is unique. It is like a sandwich, but it is smaller and tastier, complete with bread rolls from heaven and filled with a variety of ingredients that range from cured meats to fish. The *montadito* predates the sandwich too, and so this is an ancient tradition in Spain and most notably in Andalucía. It's a bite-sized slice of heaven that offers an incredible payoff for something so small and modest.

Victor then pointed to the man making the food on the other side of the kitchen window. His name was José Luis. He had flowing hair, a neatly manicured beard, and looked to be in remarkable shape. His sleeves were rolled up revealing a swath of tattoos as well as chiseled biceps. He didn't smile, but rather offered an acknowledging nod before returning back to his work, cooking, grilling, baking bread, and assembling these *montaditos* that could only be fantastic based upon the smells escaping from his kitchen. His movements were very deliberate, precise almost, as he navigated the kitchen and prepared the food with the focus of a master technician.

"That's José Luis," said Victor. "Been with me since he was twelve years old. He's an artist in the kitchen. He comes up with everything on the menu on his own."

Like many families, José Luis' had been in Cádiz for many years, centuries even. And he could trace his bloodlines back nearly as far as Ancient Rome it seemed. They were entrenched in the fabric of the city, and they had never left. He had a brother, two sisters, and a mother in town. His father had worked on the fishing boats for many years until one day his heart gave out with no warning. He was not an old man, but he had lived a hard life and had done hard work. He didn't believe in limits, and so he had worked beyond them. In doing so, he had departed far too early. The family was crushed. Boys, after all, need their fathers, and José Luis was only nine years old when his father died.

From a young age, José Luis had exhibited a talent for *fútbol*, a raw talent, and he could always be found dribbling a ball over the ancient cobblestone streets. Victor would see him outside the restaurant, and José Luis would pass the ball to him. The ball was an extension of José Luis, of his will, his soul, his dreams. It never seemed to get away from him, and he summoned it to comply with his wishes, as if he had been born with the ball at his feet. It wasn't long before he was playing in the Cádiz CF academy as a youth player, and there was even talk that Real Madrid would make an offer while he was still in his teens. He was that good, and it seemed there wasn't anything that would stop him from fulfilling his destiny as a footballer. He dreamed of playing in the great stadiums, and his family eagerly awaited the day when he would ease their burdens and sign his first professional contract.

"What happened?" I asked Victor.

"Ultimately, it was not to be," said Victor. "One day you get in the wrong car, with the wrong person, and you wake up in a hospital room after surgery to repair a compound fracture in your leg. You wake up to see the relieved faces of family members and doctors and you feel the pain that can't be masked by medications. You ask the doctor about your chances of playing again, of being the player you once were, of recapturing your breakneck speed, and you don't need to wait for the answer when you look at his face while you are posing the question. You stop him even before he has finished trying to soften the blow and raise your open hand as you turn your eyes downward. That's it. One day. One day you get in the wrong car and the curtain falls."

Victor finished speaking. He was emotional and he took a moment to collect himself. I watched José Luis through the window, and he moved, not like a man filled with melancholy, but rather reservation—to his work, his craft, and his station in life. But he moved with pride, and it was easy to see that he remained completely focused on his work in the kitchen. This was more than a mere passing fancy and less than a calling, but he committed fully to it, giving his attention to every last detail.

"Do you have any kids?" I asked Victor in hopes of steering the conversation in a different direction.

"*Tengo cuatro hijas*," he replied. "Fifteen, thirteen, twelve, and nine."

"*Cuatro!*" I said dumbfounded. "That's incredible. Congratulations."

"It's a blessing," said Victor. "They are all healthy, and it's a blessing. They are intelligent and beautiful— thankfully taking after their mother. You?"

"I have two sons," I said. "They are good boys and they take good care of each other and have their backs like only brothers can. It is, as you said, a blessing."

"Always wanted to have a son," said Victor. "José Luis is the closest I've got. I've tried to support him since those days when he was dribbling on the cobblestone and since that day he asked if there was anything he could do to earn a little money. Told him he could start out cleaning floors and toilets, and he didn't hesitate for a minute."

It was hard to imagine Victor as a father of daughters. He was so incredibly masculine, swarthy almost, a real man's man. Short with his words. Terse. A little rough around the edges. However, the more he talked about José Luis, the more he revealed a soft underbelly. The machismo, ultimately, was more of a facade, albeit a convincing one. His heart might have appeared to be constructed from the same unflinching stone that lined the walls in Cádiz, but it didn't take much for it to soften. This, by no means made him soft. If anything, it increased his protective instincts, and I pitied the man who would one day ask Victor for one of his daughter's hands in marriage or the man who, dare I say, did one of them wrong.

I looked over the menu in an attempt to decide what to eat, but it wasn't easy. It wasn't easy because the list of *montaditos* was endless. Shrimp, chicken, beef, pork, tuna, squid and on and on it went. Flavors and spices and olive oil. There were so many choices, and I wanted to get it right. I wanted to make the right choice, with the great smell wafting out of the kitchen and José Luis moving methodically in front of the grill. After much consternation, I ordered two *montaditos* with *gambas* (shrimp). After all, we were by the sea in Cádiz, surrounded by water, in the place where Columbus had set out, and José Luis' father had been a fisherman. And so, it only seemed fitting to choose something that had emerged from this vast body of water. It was a good choice, Victor confirmed, an appropriate choice, and I eagerly awaited the *montaditos*, while Victor went back to give José Luis the order and loosely assist with the preparation.

As I drank my beer, I could hear the conversation of the women at the table next to the bar. I wasn't nosy. I kept to my own business, and I didn't like to eavesdrop. But the place was small and with Victor in the back, their voices were now the only sound to be heard. They seemed wholly unaffected by my presence, perhaps convinced that my Spanish wasn't good enough to decipher what they were saying or else they simply didn't care if I heard their conversation or wanted me to hear it. Regardless, the words flowed out of their mouths and into my ears.

The woman sitting with her back to the wall was tall. She was tall and lean and dressed in a fine coat with an elegant magenta scarf around her neck. She had dark skin and neatly cropped light hair. She was in her late forties and went to great lengths not to appear as if she was still in her twenties or thirties. The woman across from her was likely a decade older, dressed a bit less stylish in hopes of appearing a decade younger it seemed. There was a slight roguishness about her, with long hair and a loud voice that easily filled the small space.

"Can you believe the news?" said the older woman.

"It is shocking," said the younger woman. "I really can't believe Cristina did it."

"They say she didn't tell a soul, that she didn't breathe a word of it to anyone," said the older woman.

"I have to say I never thought she would do it," said the younger woman. "I know there had been rumors about him for years, but even so."

"Well, I certainly don't feel sorry for him," said the older woman. "Whatever public humiliation he suffers is well deserved."

"How long do you think she planned it?" said the younger woman. "It was very well thought out. Don't you think?"

"Yes, it was," said the older woman. "I really admire her. And truth be told, I didn't think she had it in her."

I learned a lot about Cristina in only a few minutes. Like many women her age in Spain, Cristina had given up her own career aspirations for her husband. She had given up the opportunity to go to a university in Madrid in order to remain close to home. And she gave up on the possibility of being a lawyer to make a home for their family and raise their children in Cádiz. Although she enjoyed being a mother, it wasn't lost on her that she had forfeited something, that there had been sacrifices, and she was left wondering if they had been worth it.

"The way she did it was very smart," said the younger woman. "It was cunning and smart, and I admire her."

"I do too," said the older woman. "I didn't know that Cristina was so cunning and smart; she kept those traits well hidden, but then vengeance is a powerful motivator."

"Can you imagine the look on his face?" said the younger woman. "It really must have been something."

"And the look on the faces of the women?" said the older woman. "To find themselves at the hotel room at the same time!"

"The effort to clue in their husbands was the real stroke of genius," said the younger woman. "What a scene it must have been! I never would have guessed, but sometimes people really do get what they deserve."

"It doesn't happen often," said the older woman.

Victor came out from the kitchen and served me my *montaditos*. They looked as good as they smelled. The bread was warm and fresh, toasted, and bathed in olive oil. I carefully grabbed the first *montadito* with both hands and raised it to my mouth. I was not disappointed. The *gambas* were grilled and seasoned to perfection, and the heads had even been removed. This was not always common in Spain, and many times you received your *gambas* with the heads attached, the face of the sea creature frozen in time from the moment that fate imposed its will. My wife didn't like ordering *gambas* in Spain because of this. She didn't like seeing the heads attached and she was even less interested in removing them herself. However, this did not bother me. It did not bother me to see the head, and I wasn't deterred by eating the insides either. I felt more like a real man of the sea, tougher, somehow more rugged and manly for not needing the *gambas* prepared in more pristine fashion. It was as if I was saying, give them to me with the head on a platter, and I will devour the very innards. It didn't seem so different from the manner in which Cristina had served up her husband. And there was something savage and satisfying about it.

"This is incredible," I said to Victor. "A masterpiece really. How can something so simple taste so good?"

"José Luis will never tell," said Victor. "He won't even tell me. He only says that he enjoys seeing the customers happy and that he never wants to let them down. In twenty years, he never has."

I sat in the corner of the small restaurant. I was in Cádiz, once home to the Phoenicians, the place where Columbus embarked upon two of his journeys to the New World. It was late, and I was tired, but I wished the night could last forever, that the sun refused to rise, and that the world could stand still for just a moment. I watched the people outside the restaurant bring their cigarettes to their mouths, and I saw a string of smoke stand out against the blackness of the night sky.

Victor stood at the bar once again, leaning on his right elbow, with his shirt unbuttoned at the top. He arched back and took a quick look over his shoulder, through the window, approvingly, at José Luis. José Luis didn't even lift his head. He just kept working. There were no more customers to be served, and he was now cleaning the grill, scraping off the residue meticulously. He was indeed an artist, as Victor had surmised. A reluctant one it seemed but an artist, nonetheless. Still, I couldn't help but think that he certainly didn't get what he deserved. He turned on the faucet in the kitchen to wash his hands. Victor took a cigarette out of his shirt pocket and lit it as if celebrating a victory. The women at the table were now laughing, toasting Cristina presumably, hoisting their glasses over and over, as the night wore on and I ate *montaditos* by the sea in Cádiz.

# STREET LEVEL

---

The Thai restaurant in Granada was easy to miss. It was wedged between a coffee shop and a hair salon with nothing but a small sign above the door in nondescript block letters. We might not have even noticed it were it not for the whirring motor of the scooter that was constantly coming and going, slipping nimbly between buildings to pick up orders and deliver them throughout the city.

The delivery driver was impossible to miss. He always got our attention, as he seemed to perform small miracles maneuvering in tight spaces. Scooters are common in Granada, but he shared little in common with the average person riding a scooter. He took more risks, cut more corners, and rode with an attitude that seemed to show little regard for his body's safe return. This was obvious in watching him slide his tires skillfully around a turn, as his long hair flew out from beneath his helmet. It was clear he knew the streets, and at times he rode as if he owned them, not so much in an arrogant way as a comfortable one, like a man completely relaxed in his own living room. Truth be told, it was inspiring, a spectacle all its own, and we watched his scooter thread the needle outside the Thai restaurant time and time again.

Inside the external glass doors, the Thai restaurant was long and narrow. There were no tables, just a long countertop with white plastic barstools where we could sit and watch our food be cooked, eat at the counter, or just wait patiently if we were taking our food to go. At the end of the bar, there was a tall refrigerator with the Coca-Cola logo featured on the side that was for drinks only, and we were free to select what we wanted to drink and pay for it later. The Thai restaurant was a good spot, and we were glad we lived nearby.

Since we lived just around the corner, there was no reason to have our food delivered. We nearly always took our food to go, and this provided us with time waiting at the restaurant as our food was being prepared. This allowed us to get to know the staff quite well, and nearly all of them knew us by name. All of them except the man who was responsible for making the deliveries on his scooter. We caught glimpses of him coming and going, said hello, and exchanged simple pleasantries, but our interactions never extended beyond that.

"His name is Samuel," one of the cooks, Héctor, informed us. "He's quiet. *Tranquilo.* Bit of a loner. But nobody rides a scooter like him. He can get more food delivered in a night on these ancient streets than anyone. Have you seen him ride?"

"He's incredible," I said. "Every time he returns, I think he is going to crash through the glass doors, but I get the feeling he could slide between the barstools if he wanted to."

"You're just about right," said Héctor, almost laughing in agreement.

One aspect of the Thai restaurant that was unique is that it was run entirely by men. Just men. In fact, in all our time there, we never once saw a female employee. Never. There was nothing uncomfortable about this, but it was noticeable. It was also just different not seeing a single woman working there. We never learned any reason for this, but it gave the Thai restaurant an air of raw masculinity that was uncommon, even in patriarchal Spain.

Moreover, the restaurant wasn't just run by men. It was run by the toughest looking men we had seen in Granada. Most men in Granada dressed with casual elegance. They took great care regarding their appearance. They wore shirts with collars and their hair was always perfectly manicured. You didn't see lots of T-shirts and goatees and tattoos.

The men at the Thai restaurant were different, completely different. Most of them were big and swarthy and had their skin covered with tattoos to go along with nose rings and other visible piercings. They looked more hardened and outwardly intimidating. This might sound negative or stereotypical but, for displaced American expats from Los Angeles, it was comforting. It was comforting, and it made us feel like we weren't so far from home.

And the guys at the Thai restaurant would have fit in seamlessly in Los Angeles. In some way, everyone fits in Los Angeles, even if you don't fit in anywhere else. That was always part of the city's appeal for me. But nobody would have been surprised if the guys at the Thai restaurant said they were from Compton or South Central or East Los, and they seemingly made no efforts to conform to the manicured, societal norms of Andalucía. Maybe that was what we identified with more the anything—the refusal to conform to society's expectations, a touch of unapologetic rebellion. Los Angeles, after all, is nothing if not unapologetic.

One thing we knew for certain was that we fit in at the Thai restaurant, and we fit in with the guys who worked there. We fit in with them more than we did with the typical *Granadino* and more than we did with the other American expats in Granada. We weren't sure we truly fit in anywhere in Granada but, sitting on plastic barstools inside the Thai restaurant, we felt as much at home as anywhere else.

The Thai restaurant also satisfied our cravings for excellent Thai food—which wasn't easy to come by in Granada. Pad Thai, spring rolls, and all types of other dishes. In addition to the food, the guys that worked there were generous, truly generous. They customized the dishes for us, and even had us try different variations they thought we might like based upon our previous selections. We were good customers, very good customers, and it wasn't long before they knew our standard orders when we walked in the door.

There were not a lot of Americans in Granada, and the guys at the restaurant liked to ask us about living in the States, but they really wanted to know about LA. It was more than a curiosity for them, closer to a fascination, and none of them had ever been to Los Angeles.

In Spain, everyone wants to know about Los Angeles. It's LA, after all, and it signifies the entertainment capital of the world, even a world away. Hollywood, in particular, still holds a nostalgic romanticism that likely disappeared years ago. But for people in Spain who have never been to Los Angeles, the glorious image of a parade of endless movie stars lives on. It holds a real allure, and the guys at the Thai restaurant were no different. They were always eager to hear any LA story we had to offer while the noodles simmered in oil and they cooked our food. We had lots of them, since everyone from Los Angeles has a traffic story, a celebrity story, and a gun story. They looked forward to hearing a new one each time.

Although they spoke almost no English, they were always happy to converse and stumble through conversations with our limited Spanish. Unlike some verbal interactions with people in Granada that could be stressful or frustrating, it was always fun with the guys at the Thai restaurant. I told them they were my professors of *Español*, and they informed me that title had never been bestowed upon them before. "*Sí!*" I said. "*Es verdad*," and they laughed. "You hear that?" Héctor would call out to his *compañeros*. "Please refer to me now as Professor Héctor López Sánchez."

We took out food from their restaurant multiple times a week, and we really were the definition of regulars. Moreover, the guys at the Thai place always ensured that we felt welcome in such a manner that almost made us forget we were in Spain. This wasn't easy, as living abroad can be isolating. But that is how the guys made us feel. They made us feel at home, and we liked going there very much.

Over the course of an entire year in Granada, we met lots of nice people, and we crossed paths with good families. But we were never invited over to a Spanish family's home for dinner. Not a single time. Despite the many pleasantries we exchanged and the small, lovely interactions that took place, there were limitations to our ability to integrate, really integrate, quickly. Our friend Raúl, who was from Spain, said this was very common.

Raúl had an excellent perspective, since he had lived in the United States for a number of years before returning to Spain.

"When I moved to the United States," Raúl said "everyone on the street welcomed me with open arms and invited me over to dinner. I thought this was really nice, but the truth is, most never invited me over again. It was nothing more than a gesture. In Spain, it might take you two years to be welcomed into a family's home, but once you are, you are like family. You'll be invited for life. It's just different here."

This was comforting, although it was hard to know if this was entirely accurate or just a way for Raúl to make us feel better. Either way, it did make us feel slightly better. After all, we had only lived in Granada for ten months, which was still a relatively short amount of time.

In the springtime, the snow began to melt off the beautiful Sierra Nevada mountains and the air temperatures started to warm up. Even when the sun went down, it was very comfortable, and we enjoyed eating on the rooftop patio of our small apartment. It was lovely, and we could see everything, from the edge of the Alhambra Palace to the mountains to the soaring Granada

Cathedral—each extending above a beautiful blanket of red rooftops as the sun began to dip. It was a pretty magnificent setting, and we sat on the roof whenever possible.

On one of our last nights in Granada, we decided to order Thai food and eat on the roof. I went downstairs, placed the order, and paid for it. It was truly a beautiful night, with an apocalyptic sunset rolling in. With our time in Granada coming to an end, I felt inspired to order nearly everything on the menu it seemed. I figured we would eat the leftovers the next day. When the guys at the restaurant packed the food up, it became readily apparent that it would take more than two hands to get the food to our apartment. I was about to text our eldest son to come down and help when Samuel stopped me and said, "*No pasa nada. Te ayudaré.*"

Since we lived so close to the restaurant, it was never necessary for Samuel to hop on his scooter and deliver to our flat. I would sometimes chat briefly with Samuel when he returned to pick up more food before setting out in search of the next delivery location. But these interactions were brief, very brief, and it was hard to get a keen sense of him in the little time we had shared. Still, his offer was generous. It was generous, and it was clear to see that it was genuine.

Samuel had a slight frame, with that long hair that peeked out from beneath his helmet, and a tattoo that ran down his arm and another at the base of his neck. He wasn't physically imposing, but there was something quiet and introspective about him. And there was both an inner strength and a fragility in him that sat below the surface. You certainly wouldn't have ever picked up on it watching him slice through the narrow streets. But there was something a little more complex about Samuel. Although he was young, he had been given a face that looked like he had lived a dozen lifetimes, with steady eyes that could look right through you. It was clear Samuel was an observer, a thinker, and you always had the sense that he was perceptive if not talkative.

Although I told him it wasn't necessary for him to help me carry all of the food, he insisted. Samuel knew we were good customers, and he had observed the authentic, if cumbersome, banter that existed between us and the guys who worked at the restaurant. He was always observing it seemed.

Samuel and I walked across the street with bags in both hands and entered through the heavy, green door at the base of our building. After climbing four sets of stairs, I gave Samuel a tip and invited him inside the apartment. "Come on in," I said. "Thanks so much once again. You are welcome to have a drink with us or a quick bite. We have plenty of food as you know."

"Thank you," he said. "But I can't. I am working, and there will be more deliveries to make tonight."

I nodded respectfully, but I was able to convince him to come upstairs to the rooftop and say hello to my wife and kids. He knew my wife a bit from the number of times she ordered take out, since he would see her waiting at the counter as he came back and forth from his deliveries. All of the guys at the restaurant liked her. She was very comfortable with them, more comfortable with them than nearly anyone in Granada. They never made her feel bad about her limited Spanish or the fact that she liked to wear tennis shoes or that she had special orders. Every interaction had a real kindness and they were warm and welcoming. Not everyone in Granada was warm and welcoming, but the guys at the Thai restaurant were. And we were glad Samuel agreed to climb the spiral stairs to the rooftop deck and say hello.

People in Granada pride themselves in conducting themselves with an unnerving amount of composure. They rarely look surprised, and they almost never seem to possess a sense of genuine awe. After all, they live near the Alhambra Palace, so providing them with a sight that takes their breath away is no small challenge. Their eyes aren't easy to catch off-guard, and so Samuel's response was unexpected. He stopped and took a deep breath, then exhaled as if he had just shed a hundred tons of weight, as if his soul had been set free. If I was being romantic, I might have even categorized his response as emotional. "Incredible," he said. "It's beautiful. I have never seen this view before. I live on the streets, on my scooter, year after year, day and night, and I do my job and I know this city. But nobody has ever invited me up. I have seen this city over and over, for years and years but I have never seen *this* city."

Samuel said hello to my wife and our sons, and he extended his hand graciously. He was very cognizant of not disrupting our dinner, but his presence was just the opposite. We told him the Thai restaurant was our favorite restaurant in Granada, and it was our pleasure to have him over. In fact, it was something of an honor. He was our guest, and we reiterated again that he could stay if he was able. At first, he shook his head "no," reiterating that he had other deliveries to follow. Samuel then took a moment of quiet contemplation and decided to allow himself one beer. "*Vale*," he said. "*Una cerveza.*"

"*Gracias*," he said genuinely appreciative.

"*No pasa nada*," I replied, using my favorite expression Spaniards use in response to simple generosities. As he drank his beer, he walked around the small rooftop deck in order to fully absorb the vastly different views in each direction. Each day, he rode his scooter to work and parked it on the street below our building. He climbed off the bike with his slight frame, removed his helmet carefully, walked through the sliding glass doors of the Thai restaurant and then shuttled food all over the city, traversing every curve and bend in the road, tempting fate just inches from the stone buildings that can leap out and knock a rider off their bike. It never happened to Samuel. He could feel the ground, the road. He could calculate the distance between himself and the walls, and he knew the surface beneath his tires. He understood its characteristics, and he knew just how his scooter would react. He could feel it in his bones, and he lived his life there.

"Thank you ... for this," he reiterated. "Most people," his voice trailing off slightly. "Most people choose to meet me at street level."

Now he stood four stories above street level, alongside an unlikely American family, during one of our final days in Granada as the last rays of sun hit his face and the day turned to night and the Alhambra lit up and the lights began to turn on inside houses embedded in the side of the hill. He was Spanish to the core, a true *Granadino*, and something of an urban legend on these streets. We were Americans adrift in Spain. Together we looked out over the once unrivaled Moorish kingdom with beers in our hands, feeling as though everything as far as the eye could see ... was ours.

# THE CONGESTED
# WAITER

It was mid-morning when we appeared at the breakfast buffet at the hotel in Portugal. The hotel was in the Algarve overlooking the Pacific Ocean, and we woke to find ourselves extremely hungry. It was easy to be hungry on the coast of Portugal, with an array of fresh seafood at our disposal and the nicely prepared dishes with local flavors and lots of style and panache.

The hotel was bustling in the morning. They had a wonderful buffet spread, and it was nice to get away and enjoy a breakfast that included everything from eggs and oatmeal to waffles and fruit. Our teenage boys had bottomless stomachs now, and this also seemed to be the economically efficient way of doing things when it came to food consumption.

The breakfast dining room was lovely, with floor to ceiling windows and doors, the morning light streaming in, and great, sweeping views of the coastline. It was something out of a movie, and families arrived at breakfast each morning in well-thought-out clothes arrangements that oozed style, with the day before them and all the accessories needed to conquer it.

We arrived in flip-flops. Nobody in our family was carrying a parasol or wearing an Armani suit or even a polo shirt. We were in Europe, but we might not have been considered Europeans quite yet. T-shirts and gym shorts were more our speed, and so we might have called attention to ourselves due to our relatively pedestrian wardrobes. However, this wasn't the South of France. This was Portugal, a beautiful collision of cultures, and there is room in Portugal for everyone.

Portugal, in itself, is such a wonderful contradiction. Although the Portuguese people are known to have a bit of melancholy in their affect and persona, this is in stark contrast to the explosive, electric colors that adorn buildings and the delectable foods that tantalize the palate.

Of course, there is more than a touch of sadness in the beautiful fado music that teems out into the streets at night in the city of Lisbon. But there is a grace that accompanies the music that is as much a celebration of life as anything. Down here in the Algarve, things were a bit different. It was a resort area, after all, but it maintained enough elements that were distinctly Portuguese.

The staff at the hotel worked incredibly hard in the mornings, tasked with the challenge of accommodating so many people in the dining room at one time. They assembled a virtual army of employees, and they moved with an urgency you weren't likely to find in neighboring Spain. I wouldn't go as far as to say they were hustling, but they were attentive, and it was clear they put forth a real effort on behalf of the hotel guests.

Davi was in his fifties. He was slightly overweight, with dark hair that was often disheveled and eyes as black as night. He had been working at the hotel for twenty-seven years, long before he had a family of his own and long before he possessed the fairly good-sized belly he now toted around. It wasn't difficult to see that he would have been quite handsome as a young man, before age and time and life had begun to erode his looks.

When he started there, he was quite a young man and he was very eager. He was trying to earn money to help his younger siblings, and he was always looking to take double shifts or do anything that had the potential to earn him a bit of extra money. He did, and it seemed like he was there all the time. It was a sacrifice, but it was one Davi had been willing to make. Nearly three decades on, that sacrifice had taken its toll, but he never complained, and he would tell you it had been worth it if asked.

In those days, those younger days, when Davi was roguishly handsome, he smoked lots of cigarettes and probably drank too much as well. He felt like he was invincible and, truth be told, he was young enough to get away with it. However, that was many years ago. Times change. Men grow up (or try to) and he couldn't get away with that now. For starters, his wife would crucify him, but it was more than that. He was older now. Much older. His body was older now, and it simply couldn't handle it. His constitution had changed, and he tried to take better care of himself, despite the fact that it often looked like just the opposite. In fact, at times, it looked as if Davi simply neglected his own well-being. The weight gain had a lot to do with that perception. It always does, and Davi had gained quite a lot of weight in recent years. However, this wasn't due so much to hard living, but rather the result of a changing metabolism combined with quitting cigarettes after years of smoking two packs a day.

I got to know Davi during our stays at the hotel. We stayed there as a family, but perhaps Davi could identify with the fatigue he saw in us each morning, juggling the challenges of parenthood even when on vacation. We weren't the typical family at the hotel to be sure—bejeweled, with neatly manicured nails, and new haircuts. We certainly weren't that. We were more likely to stumble out of bed, continuously chasing family life only to find ourselves a few steps behind.

I suspect Davi realized this early on. We showed more battle scars than the average vacationing family, and Davi picked up on our willingness to lay ourselves bare. For his part, he always tried to greet us with a smile at breakfast, but he also made sure not to raise his voice too loud—almost as if he was talking to someone who might have been hungover. This was something I really liked about Davi. There was a kindness and a gentleness about him. An awareness. A discreetness. I liked that he was perceptive, intuitive almost, with an understanding of just when he might have needed to raise his voice or when the situation required he lower it.

One morning, as he took drink orders and carried plates to and from the kitchen, I noticed that Davi was terribly congested. He sneezed more than once and seemed to have a chest cold as well. Davi tried his best to hide it, but it was impossible to conceal such a visible, outward illness. There was nothing he could do to disguise it, and any efforts to do so were relatively futile. From the perspective of hotel guests, it is never an encouraging sign to have a congested waiter, particularly when they are handling plates and cups and utensils. And Davi was nothing if not congested that morning. He was terribly congested, complete with an errant, runny nose and the kind of conspicuous cough that only emerges in big men, who summon greater sounds from their large bodies when they are ill. It was a disturbing, unappetizing sight to witness. He was clearly battling and had come down with something nasty. There was no question about it.

I wouldn't necessarily go as far as to say that Davi and I had become close friends, at least not in the traditional sense. We didn't correspond regularly throughout the year, and there was very much an out of sight, out of mind quality to our relationship. But there was something meaningful there. We had gotten to know one another pretty well over the years. I got to know him first as a guest at the hotel, and he got to know me (or at least observed me) in the same role. But there was a genuine kinship from the beginning, an easy understanding between men, even if it was born in a somewhat stilted manner through these pleasant, professional interactions. But I really got to know Davi outside of the hotel.

Whenever my family and I came to stay at the hotel, Davi and I always made plans to grab a drink off the property. Davi knew this little place where we were certain not to run into any of the hotel guests (or staff for that matter) and this was the only place we frequented together. It wasn't a place that would have appealed to the upper end of society, and it was the kind of place you wouldn't just show up unless you knew someone, or someone brought you there. This was a place that existed independent of any licenses that might have been required to create and run such an establishment. It was off the radar and, I am quite certain, off the books.

The entrance was no more than a door. A door that could have been anywhere, on any street—home to a family or diplomat or dry-cleaner or thief. It was outside of the city center, slightly off the beaten path with no signage—just a door that could have led anywhere. It was run by a woman. She knew Davi, and when he entered, she said hello in a manner that suggested she might have had an interest that extended beyond his patronage. He responded warmly but cautiously, with considerably less enthusiasm than she showed. This always seemed to disappoint her, but it also seemed necessary for Davi to communicate from the first word exactly where they stood.

On the surface, the interior of the place was a classic bar. Dark. Musty. It was filled with smoke and dim lights that adorned the walls around the outside as well as a couple of lamps that swung over billiard tables. But the bar wasn't light fare. It wasn't the type of place where old friends meet at the end of the day, but more likely one where people came to settle old debts ... and incur new ones I would imagine. The place carried a lot of baggage, real weight, and if you found yourself there at the end of a day, there was probably little chance that anything positive would come from it. Still, for the two of us, it served its purpose. Davi would never run into a coworker there, and so it offered him the chance to be discreet about our friendship and not seem like he was cavorting around town with one the hotel guests or providing us with special treatment during our stays.

"Morning, Davi," said my wife, as he glided over to our table, still possessing a touch of the smoothness that was more reminiscent of his youth. "Have you come down with a cold?" she asked innocently enough.

"I have," said Davi. "My apologies. I had hoped I could hide it."

"You poor thing," said my wife sympathetically. "You should be in bed getting some rest, Davi."

"Well, I have to pay the bills," he remarked. "We have three kids now and another on the way."

"Congratulations," I chimed in. "I didn't know that your wife was expecting again."

"How wonderful, Davi," exclaimed my wife. "Absolutely wonderful news. Please congratulate your wife as well."

Of course, my wife knew all about my friendship with Davi. She had only met his wife once, when his wife worked at the hotel a number of years ago before they were married. Our off-site friendship didn't include the wives. My wife was OK with that. More than OK, in fact. She encouraged it. I had always been more of a loner, and she had been telling me I needed more male friends since the day we met. She still enjoyed time with her girlfriends, while I had become more of a recluse as the years wore on. Work life and family life were busy enough, and besides that, our sons were now old enough that any needs I might have had for male bonding were more than met on a regular basis by them.

"Thank you both," said Davi. "We are excited. I am just trying to shake this cold. You know how it is with a house full of kids and germs. Always trying to shake a cold."

"Absolutely," I said. "I feel for you."

"Of course, Davi," said my wife. "It's hard to stay healthy with kids," she remarked. However, my wife wasn't buying his story. He was run down, worn down, she thought, and she sensed something wasn't quite right with his response.

I pretty much trusted everyone I met, or at least gave them the benefit of the doubt. I was an honest person, and I expected others to be the same. If they told me something, I believed it. My wife was different. In fact, she was the opposite, not regarding her own honesty. She was honest to the core, but she wasn't convinced this was the norm, that honesty was human nature. Trust didn't come naturally to her, and people had to prove themselves worthy of her trust if they had any hopes of obtaining it. It wasn't something she doled out easily. She also had good intuition to go along with her own keen perceptive abilities, and on this morning, she was convinced, wholly convinced, that Davi wasn't telling us the truth. When we got back to our room, she remarked "Davi was obviously lying. I wonder what is going on with him. I know you are meeting him tonight. Perhaps you can learn more."

Davi and I had planned to grab a drink that evening. We met, as we always did, in the main center of the town of Lagos. From there, Davi would drive us to the bar, which I would never have been able to find in a million years. It was away from the populated areas but not so far that I would have considered it remote. I wasn't blessed with a great sense of direction, so it was difficult for me to determine precisely where this bar was located, but there were more twists and turns than I could ever have navigated successfully. These shortcomings combined with the fact that the bar was concealed even beyond the recognition of people who passed it day after day would have made it impossible for me to get there on my own.

When I got in Davi's car, I noticed he was more anxious than normal. He was almost jumpy, as if he had just had three cups of coffee or was hopped up on something. Since I always knew him to be extraordinarily calm, this was particularly noticeable.

"Everything alright?" I asked.

"I am OK," he said. "Still under the weather."

This sounded less than convincing, and I was beginning to think my wife was right. We drove in the dark, from the town center of Lagos and into the Portuguese darkness. Portugal always seemed to have a tinge of darkness, even in the daylight hours. It really is a remarkably beautiful country, but the Portuguese people do carry themselves with something just a little bit somber, more knowing. It is almost as if they have seen too much, been through too much, to be buoyant and free of worry. They enjoy life, but they respect its ability to humble them at any moment. This takes just a small amount of the sheen away, and the people of Portugal are often unable to match the vibrancy of their buildings.

Davi was much like this. He was intelligent. He had charisma, and style didn't elude him. He was charming and affable, but the sadness behind his eyes was inescapable. It couldn't be hidden by an easy smile or sidestepped by a kind word. Tonight, his inner uneasiness was even more visible, magnified with him being so congested. His cold was affecting his appearance, now having authored in large bags under his eyes. He looked a bit more like a man on the edge than a family man expecting his fourth child. This concerned me, and I made a point to tell him so.

"Davi, I am concerned about you. It's important that you take care of yourself," I said. "Especially now that you have a fourth child on the way. Your family is counting on you."

Davi looked slightly annoyed at my efforts to remind him of the size of his increasing responsibilities in a somewhat patronizing manner. But he snapped out of it quickly and straightened up in the driver's seat as he shifted the car into fourth gear.

"You're right," he said. "Sorry. Not trying to bring the night down. It's good to see you, old friend. It's always good to see you. Everything will be alright. Thanks for making the time to catch up."

"Of course, Davi' I said. "I am sure everything will be alright."

Davi drove expertly into the night. He had shifted the gears of the car, shifted the mood, and returned to something of his old self despite the congestion and whatever other issues he was dealing with. He was clearly in character now, playing his role expertly, as we drove up to the bar and parked his car on the street.

"It will be good to get that drink, yes?" he said with a smile.

"Yes, it will," I said. "It certainly will."

"Let's go in," said Davi amiably.

We stepped out of the car. The place was barely lit, with just one small light on the outside of the building. It didn't look like a place seeking customers as much as a refuge for lonesome travelers heading down a long, lonely road. However, as we walked across the gravel stones and toward the door, it looked more like a safehouse than an oasis.

When we walked in the door, Davi drew a number of heavy glances his way. The bartender eyed him carefully while polishing glasses, and we sat down on two barstools directly in front of her.

"Two beers please," announced Davi almost ceremoniously. "For my friend and I!"

As I looked around the bar, it was eerily quiet. It certainly didn't seem like people were going to raise a glass to Davi, the bartender included. I could go as far as to say that Davi might not have even been welcome there, were it not for the fact that he brought me along with him. The bar was obviously comprised of people who were no strangers to the place, and Davi seemed to gain some sort of protection from bringing me along. I can't say that I didn't feel used, but I was getting past my own hurt feelings quickly with the sense that Davi was in some real trouble and that whatever trouble he found himself in might have been justification enough. Most of all, I was just worried about him, and it was clear by the looks around the room that I probably had good reason to be concerned.

"*Obrigado*," Davi said to the bartender with gratitude upon receiving our beers.

The bartender said nothing, and handed our beers over as if she was in a hurry to be rid of them, almost as if the very act of serving us might classify her as an accessory to whatever Davi was involved in.

"Cheers," said Davi. "To friendship."

"To friendship," I repeated.

"As you might imagine by now," said Davi, "I am in a bit of trouble. A tight spot, as you Americans might say. It's my fault. I deserve it. Nothing too original here. It's an old story, but I owe a sizable amount of money to the wrong kind of people."

He paused for a long moment.

"It isn't just that I owe," he said. "It is that the time has come for them to collect—one way or the other."

We sat at the bar drinking our beers, savoring them a bit. I didn't say a word. I was thinking. The beer was cold and good. It was cold and it tasted good going down my throat. I wasn't always a beer drinker, but I had developed a taste for it over time. The flavors were as important as the temperature, and the beer was smooth and cold and refreshing. We drank it almost entirely in silence, inside the musty bar, in front of the quiet bartender and the hushed room with all of the eyes fixed in our direction.

There wasn't much for me to say. At this point, it was of little consequence to me how Davi found himself in this jam. My guess was he lost it at the tables. He liked the dice, and I could see him gambling as an outlet from the pressures of parenthood and a family life. Truth is, I didn't really care what Davi had done to get himself jammed up. I am not even sure I wanted to know. He was my friend. He was a man with more compassion than most, and I liked him. I liked him a lot.

We could have sat there for hours and Davi would never have asked me to help. He wasn't going to ask me for one cent, and I knew it. He had too much pride to ask, and he would take it on the chin if he had to. But I also knew he would be grateful if I offered. After all, he had brought me there, and he had confessed his situation to me. Deep down, I knew he was hoping I might be able to help him, much as he was ashamed to ask for my help in this regard. We knew each other and we were always comfortable sharing things about our lives, but we came from different worlds, and I never had the sense that I was one of his closest friends. Perhaps I had misjudged this. But my guess was, if I was sitting with him here, on this night at this time, it must have been a last resort. Either that or, perhaps, he feared for the friend who helped him out. I couldn't be sure.

After we finished our beers, I inquired, "How much?"

"Twenty-five thousand euros," said Davi.

"What?!" I said. "Davi. Damn." Davi didn't have any money. He lived check to check and he likely couldn't have cobbled up five thousand euros, let alone twenty-five. My heart sank.

If you have ever felt the compulsion to do something you knew would be against your better judgment, you know how I felt. It made no rational sense for me to even think about giving Davi the money, that much money, and yet I knew almost immediately that I would. Reason didn't come in to play, wouldn't come in to play—even if I couldn't be sure that Davi wasn't playing me for a con. I was a sucker, an easy mark, but I was also his friend. I trusted Davi, believed in Davi even if every fiber of my body told me to walk away. I wanted to give Davi the money, and I was going to give him the money. I was hardly a wealthy man, but I could do it. I knew it was generous, far too generous, but it felt good to help him, to be able to help him.

The world was cold, but I wasn't. Through all the cynicism adulthood brings, I refused to let myself fall victim to it. I had to believe in people, in the good in people. If you don't believe in the good in people, what's the point? At the end of the day, there are really just two kinds of people. There are those that trust and those that suspect. It always seemed so much more pleasurable to trust the best in people rather than suspect the worst, and I was going to trust Davi.

"Davi," I said. "I am going to help you. I know you aren't asking, but I am going to take care of this situation. You will have the money tonight."

"I don't know what to say," he said, the color now slowly returning to his face. "You don't know how much this means. I will—"

I cut him off. I couldn't let him say it, didn't want him to say it. No, not a promise. Not a promise that had the potential to be broken. Not that. Anything but that.

"Davi, stop," I said. "There is no debt to be repaid. There are no promises to keep, and I want it that way. It's the only way. No conversation … and no strings."

"Thank you," he said quietly, while turning his head toward me at the bar with his eyes angled downward, embarrassed but relieved. "Thank you."

Davi closed out our tab, and we walked back to his car. Neither of us had said a word for several minutes. The wind was now blowing, and it made the temperature feel quite a bit colder than it actually was. We could once again hear the gravel grinding underneath our feet as we approached his car at the end of the lot.

As I began to walk around to the passenger side, I felt Davi tug on my shoulder and turn me around to hug me the way you only hug a long-lost brother you haven't seen in twenty years. The embrace was strong and fast and then Davi stepped back and patted me affectionately with an open hand in the center of my chest. He took me back to my car in the city center, and I returned to the hotel, informed my wife of what I wanted to do, and made the arrangements to wire the money that night. Against her better judgment, it was done.

The next morning our family went to breakfast at the hotel the way we always did. The kids rushed to the buffet in search of the waffle maker, while my wife and I waited for coffee and looked around the room for Davi. When the maître d' passed by, I asked him if Davi was working, and he told me that Davi had called in sick. "Thanks," I said, as he walked away.

The morning was bright and warm, and the light streamed in perfectly through the floor to ceiling windows.

We drank our coffee and stared out the glass, toward the infinite ocean swells. We were in Portugal. It was beautiful. A new day was now upon us, and I never saw Davi again.

# THE YOUNG SURFERS
# OF SOUTHERN SPAIN

In the afternoon, on the beaches of the Spanish coastline across from the shores of Morocco, the young surfers stare out at the aquamarine gloss of the Mediterranean Sea and let the hours disappear without apology. They sit on thin, beach blankets, with beers in their hands while their dogs run back and forth into the water. The bodies of the surfers are tanned and beautiful. The hair of the young men is longer than usual, much like the California surfers of the '70s, and it drapes across their faces with style. The women are lean and strong, with a few modest tattoos, meaningful inscriptions it seems, and small bikinis they could only wear flatteringly in the fleeting days of beauty and youth.

I am led in their direction by my own dog, who nearly drags me to them since he is blind but still very capable of detecting the sounds and scents of other dogs. He is also enormous, a two-hundred-pound majestic lumbering mass of English Mastiff. He is soulful, born with the burden of great size. Every movement requires heavy lifting, but his instincts are pure. They are pure and good and noble. My wife likes to say he is "like a big, cube of butter," and that's not far off. After all, he does make just about everything, well … better.

Although I am more likely to keep to myself, the dogs have other ideas. The dogs, of the young surfers, circle around my English Mastiff, and the surfers are interested as well. "What's his name," they ask along with "How old is he?" when they see all of the gray hairs around his mouth. Now their dogs are barking at him, playfully, trying to get him to engage, but they are much younger than him. He wasn't all that playful in his younger days, but now he really isn't interested. He was initially eager to sniff the other dogs, but his level of engagement ends there and the only question now is when he will determine that he has had enough. How long it will take him to communicate that he won't be plunging his hulking body into the sea.

The dogs of the young surfers have energy, surfer energy, real energy. They could go on leaping and chasing for hours, and they likely have, even before we arrived. They will not tire until they have left the beach, when they fall asleep in the back of the truck with the cool air shuttling in through the windows and the smell of the sea still lingering in the air. But, for now, their energy is boundless, and it's inspiring to watch the vigor with which they seek to draw my dog out.

Eventually, he lets out a thunderous bark that merely coincides with a lunge in the direction of one of the dogs just for emphasis. He wants to get his point across. It's forceful, and it gets the attention of a couple of topless women down the beach who sit up quickly, frightened at the intimidating sound of his bark. The decibel level is frightening, and tinged with his current level of frustration, is the ultimate conversation stopper.

The young surfers, however, are impressed. They have never seen a dog this big or this slow or one that acts this old. He is almost prehistoric, ancient, and there is a dinosaur-like quality to the way he places one foot in front of the other, a great beast prowling, roaming the earth at a time before the human race reshaped it.

"Do you live here?" I ask in an effort to make small conversation.

They nod "yes," and the tallest young man says, "We've lived here for twenty years. We are from the UK, but our parents were sick of the weather and so they moved down here."

"How do you like living here?" I ask.

"We like it," says the young woman with the shiny, dark hair that is pressed to her head, "But it has gotten so crowded."

I am from California, and I honestly don't know what she is talking about. The beach stretches out for miles, most of the sand with nobody on it, nearly uninhabited based upon my comparison being from Southern California. I have never seen so much space on a beach, so much freedom, so much privacy. Although surprised, I assume it is all relative, and I notice they set up their blankets just far enough from the *chiringuito*, which attracts tourists coming for a *tinto de verano* in the late afternoon while on holiday.

I try to play along and say, "I bet you've seen a lot of changes in the twenty years you've been here?" asking it as a question and already knowing the answer.

"You can't imagine," says the young man with the curly, brown hair drinking a beer. "When they built that port, it changed everything, the current, the surf, even the climate. Something about the way it altered the coastline seems to have impacted the ecosystem just enough to upset it. And when you add the number of people who now vacation here, it's just a bit of a drag for people who live here."

"Not sure where we can go next to get away," says the other young man with the toned, lean body and straighter hair that falls across his face. "Only place left to go is Africa," he says, which gets a half laugh from the young women even though I can tell he isn't joking.

"What about you?" asks one of the young women, trying to be polite. "Where are you from?"

"My family just moved here," I say. "We are from the US and lived in Los Angeles for the past twenty years."

"Americans," says the young man holding the beer. "We used to have a few Americans down here. Not so much anymore. They try, but they never make it here."

"Why not?" I asked, since I am both intrigued and also interested in what will apparently get the best of us.

"They can't take the inefficiency," says the young man with the hair across his face. "They see the sand and sea and eat the food and think they have found paradise. But then they realize that everything takes longer and that there is nothing they can do to speed the process up—at the post office, at a restaurant, at the doctor. They are used to things working, being solved, and getting done quickly, and they eventually become frustrated with the lifestyle here."

"Well, we came here to slow life down," I say.

They look at me, not skeptically, but rather like they have heard that before. They have seen this act play out too many times, and if I don't mind, they will reserve their judgment until a bit more time has passed. I think they sense that I am genuine, but they are going to let it play out. After all, this isn't their first rodeo.

While we talk, their dogs continue to play in the sea, the water splashing out from behind their feet, as they run through the foam and onto the sand. At my feet, my English Mastiff sits, still panting, recovering from his interaction with the other dogs. It took a lot out of him to send that message, and the walk down the beach was about as far as he could travel before needing a break.

"I hope you don't think we are rude or antisocial or just complainers," says the young woman who hasn't spoken. She is beautiful, with dark skin, light hair, and a body so perfect that you can't look at it for fear of not being able to stop looking at it. She follows up the beginning of her thought saying, "People, it's just … people."

"What about people?" I ask, making sure only to look at her eyes, which are the color of chestnuts below her tousled light brown hair.

"They just," she hesitates. "They just come down here … and ruin everything."

"How so?" I ask.

"Well," she says. "They come down here and they drink, and they party, and they build houses and condos and act like they own the place, like they have always owned the place. They come from London or Madrid or Buenos Aires, and they look down on us. They parade themselves with an air of superiority and they act as if they are never going to die."

"Well, they are going to die," I say. "Just like you and me. There is no escaping that. Even entitlement can't elude death."

"Of course," she says. "But it's the attitude that comes with that mentality. The result of this attitude is what has ultimately eroded these beaches and made them less pure than they were when we first moved here."

I know what she is saying. Of course, I understand. The young surfers here are different. They aren't hedonists. They're conservationists, purists, naturalists. They don't go to the beach to party as much as reflect. And the shoreline isn't a festive place. It's a sacred place, where nobody hurts, and people aren't supposed to trample one another. It's a place where dogs run free and play in the ocean and young surfers watch them frolic in the late afternoon sun. It's a place where the sound of the waves is rhythmic and the smell of the sea invades the nostrils with the scent of freedom, real freedom, a place where the young surfers can let the hours wash away, and the most beautiful young woman in Spain is no longer burdened by the depth of her beauty.

# THE TRIP

He had wanted to take this trip for a long time, a very long time. In fact, he had thought about it for more than four decades. Only, he didn't know where he'd be going. Still, that's a long time to consider a trip, any trip, even a hypothetical one. It's a long time to wait, and it's an even longer time to wonder. But that is what he had done. He had waited and he had wondered for all those years.

He wondered if she looked the same. He certainly didn't. She couldn't possibly, but he still wondered. Would he be able to recognize the way she turned her head haughtily? Did she still throw her chin upward in the debonair, almost arrogant manner he remembered? Did her eyes still widen with excitement at the thought of a new adventure? Oh, how her eyes would widen, how she could get excited without saying a word. He loved that about her, perhaps best of all her attributes.

This was silly, of course. All of it. A silly, childish rouse. After all, he was a man nearly seventy years old, and she couldn't have been all that much younger—in her sixties at the very least. Even the very idea that they would recognize one another was preposterous. In fact, he was certain they probably wouldn't if they were to pass on the street. And yet here he was, embarking on this trip, this trip he had waited to take for so many years, aware that his precious memories couldn't possibly remain preserved and still with that infantile enthusiasm of a schoolboy.

Sometimes he wondered if they had ever been in the same place by chance, if they had ever stepped into the same restaurant or ended up at the same bar at the end of an evening. He thought about her, and he looked for her. He looked for her in train stations and airports and when he sat down for dinner in New York or Milan or London. There was nothing that would possibly have led him to believe she would be there, that she could be there, but he always dared to hope, and he looked for her from that day on. He looked for her from the day she had left. It was a hopeless, frivolous pursuit, but he didn't care. Or perhaps he did care, but it didn't stop him from asking.

Whenever she went to a restaurant, she always requested her coat be hung up. She would ask the host if he "would be a dear" and take care of her coat until she was done eating. She said it in a way that was charming and whimsical without being flirtatious. Still, she cast a spell whenever she spoke. It was something from the movies, the old movies, movies even older than they were. By now, this request would be terribly dated. People didn't make requests that way anymore. It was dated even then. But there was a time when a request like that, spoken in just the right tone, from a woman like her, well … a man would've done just about anything if he'd heard those words.

Whenever he went to a restaurant alone, he would ask if a woman matching her description happened to be there, as if he might have had plans to meet her there. It wasn't likely. He knew that, of course, but he would ask anyways. What would be the harm, so long as he was willing to risk any embarrassment at having the maître d' say, "No, I am sorry, sir. No one matching that description has been here." He didn't mind looking as if he had been stood up. He was secure with himself. Moreover, what was a little embarrassment when the reward was so great, on the off chance she just happened to be there? Some people told him he was foolish, foolish to ask these questions and foolish to keep thinking about her after all these years. He didn't think so. "You never know," he'd say. "These things happen. Have you seen the story about the twins who were separated at birth only to be reunited years later? Life is as much about chance and luck and fate as anything else."

One evening, when he was in Madrid, he went to Sobrino de Botín, the oldest restaurant in the world. He liked to eat at Sobrino de Botín, not merely because it was the oldest in the world, but because Hemingway ate there. He loved *The Sun Also Rises*, and she did too. In addition, there was always the thought that he might glean a touch of that inspiration if he ate the roast suckling pig like Hemingway did. It was a fine restaurant, and he could see why Hemingway liked it. The walls were dark and old, brooding, and full of character. It didn't have light pouring in through a sheet of glass like the new restaurants, and he was glad they kept it this way.

As always, he asked if a woman matching her description happened to have come in before him since she said she might join him. "No sir," said the maître d'. "Interesting you should ask though, since a woman matching that description was here last night. Charming lady. We were all a bit taken by her."

For a moment, he didn't say a word. He hadn't expected this, not really, not after all these years of asking. Yes, of course, he had tried to convince his friends it might be possible. Of course, it was possible, but he hadn't really believed his own words or put a lot of thought into the possibility it might actually happen. That would simply not have been prudent, to place so much weight on something so unlikely. It was not in his nature to be impractical, and so he went on asking this question each time he entered a restaurant without emotional investment, void of sentimentality, and in a perfectly reasonable manner. This was the only way, he thought, he knew, that he could keep on asking the same question and survive.

He hadn't considered that there might actually be a time when he would receive this answer and be forced to respond. She was here, he thought, at the same time as he was. In Madrid. Was she here on business? Holiday? Perhaps she lived here. He didn't know the answer to any of these questions, but he knew how considering them made him feel. They made him feel like he was closer, perhaps closer than he had ever been, to feeling something he hadn't felt in a long time.

He cleared his head. "I … I'm sorry I missed her. I had thought we were meeting here this evening," he pretended once again.

"*Que pena*," said the maître d'. "Particularly since she said she was returning to Paris today."

"Yes. A pity," he said. "Of course. Today was the day she was planning to return to Paris," he bluffed again.

Paris, he thought. Paris surprised him. He remembered when they had traveled there together all those years ago. It was there he suggested that Paris was indeed a city for her, a city made for her, worthy of her.

She had scoffed at the idea. In fact, the very thought that he had suggested it almost offended her.

"The French are so snooty," she remarked emphatically. "I am not a bit like that. I couldn't ever see myself living there."

And yet, it seemed this was where she lived. At least, this was where she lived now. In a way, he almost felt proud. She was royalty, even without the requisite bloodlines, and he knew it. It made him happy that she might have arrived at the same conclusion.

When he landed at Charles de Gaulle Airport in Paris, he had a car waiting for him. The driver transported him to his hotel, where he unpacked his bags, showered, and changed his clothes. It was late in the afternoon now, and the sun would be starting its descent in a couple of hours. This was his favorite time of day in Paris, in the city of light, when the natural light was just about perfect and people began to leave their jobs and return home before the evening set in. At this time of day, the city embodied a genuine warmth that was not present in the early mornings or the electric nights.

He went down to the street and got in a taxi. "Bonjour," he said. "The Fifteenth Arrondissement. Square de la place du Commerce." He knew exactly where to go. How could he forget? It was the last place he had seen her, before she disappeared without so much as an explanation or a note. Oh, how she loved that little restaurant. He had returned there every night for another two weeks before he accepted the sad reality that she was gone … gone from Paris and gone from his life forever.

He opened the door of the taxi, placed one foot onto the pavement, and stepped out into the warm sunlight of the late afternoon. He paid the taxi driver and was unusually generous with the tip, more due to his preoccupation than his generosity. He was wearing a light-colored suit, perfect for summer, with a white linen shirt, no tie, and a stylish cap. The park looked just as it had all those years before—with the benches lining the outside and the flowers still in bloom. The storefronts, of course, had changed, but everything else looked pretty much the way it had the last time he was there. The restaurant had a new name, Le Commerce, but other than that seemed to be very much intact. Everything was just so, and he was comforted by the familiarity of his surroundings.

When he walked in, he spotted her immediately, and this time he wasn't surprised. She was there, at a table by the open-air window, gazing out at the park in a pantsuit befitting a woman her age. In some ways, she was unrecognizable. After all, nearly everyone is rendered unrecognizable after more than forty years. But her chin was still up—proud, haughty, laughing, mocking, or at least refusing to succumb to whatever life had brought. No. That hadn't changed. Not one bit. It was her calling card, unmistakable, and he would have recognized it anywhere.

He approached her at the side and stood next to the table. She turned calmly to face him, and he saw her eyes widen just a touch, revealing a shade of that youthfulness he recalled so well. "Madame," he said while removing his hat respectfully. "It's been a long time. Would you be a dear and invite me to sit down? I've been looking for you."

# THE JEWELER'S
# HANDS

The jeweler was in her late forties, with hair that had been dyed blonde and was shortened in a cropped, modern hairstyle that looked very flattering on a woman her age. She had flawless skin, like many women in Spain, and her complexion was fair. She was smartly dressed, with a touch of elegance, and she wore just the right amount of makeup. Every aspect of her appearance was constructed in a purposeful, attractive manner.

However, when you are a jeweler, there is nothing more important than your hands. After all, it is the hands that reach into the glass case and extract the jewelry, that lay the jewelry down on the counter or place a delicate bracelet across the delicate bones of a wrist. The jeweler's hands are always in the frame, in the sight lines of the prospective buyer. A jeweler can afford to wear blemishes anywhere but their hands, and she went to great lengths to make sure she took excellent care of them.

Some people spend their whole lives searching for their calling, but she knew she wanted to be a jeweler for nearly as long as she could remember. She wanted to be a jeweler ever since she was a little girl growing up in Barcelona. If Barcelona wasn't the economic center of Spain, it was certainly the creative center, where the presence of Gaudí loomed large, the Sagrada Familia soared, and style counted for as much as substance. If ever a city embodied the ethos of "freedom," it was Barcelona—from its Catalan core to its immense pride in being one of the great, distinct cities of the world. Even the language, which Franco worked to repress during his tenure, had survived here. This was a modern, cosmopolitan city, where culture would not give way to conformity, and the arts could thrive here, breathe here. Growing up in Barcelona influenced the jeweler very much.

She could remember the first time her mother took her to a jewelry store. Her family was not wealthy, but her mother dressed up for the occasion. She had her hair done earlier in the day, and she wore a new outfit. Although she was a relatively young girl at the time, the jeweler vividly remembered her mother's excitement that morning as they walked out the door of their small flat not far from the Sagrada Familia.

The jeweler could recall that her mother had also picked out a dress for her to wear as well. They stopped for a bite to eat at a small cafe, and her mother reminded her to try not to spill on her new dress. She had never seen her mother so preoccupied with their outward appearance, but this didn't make the girl nervous. She was very comfortable with acting refined and proper. It was all very sophisticated, and this appealed to her. It appealed to her very much. It was entirely different than the manner in which they led the rest of their lives, and it was almost as if they were setting out on a great adventure, away from the mundane quality of their daily lives, just the two of them, mother and daughter, inhabiting personas that didn't really belong to them but were on loan for the day.

Her mother took them to a jewelry store in the center of town, not far from Cataluña Square, where many of the expensive shops were located in Barcelona. When they arrived at the store, they took a moment to admire the storefront before entering. This was important to her mother. She wanted her daughter to stand there for a moment and just stare. And so, they stood in the most dignified fashion, dreaming, as they stared at the floor-to-ceiling elegant, glass window frames and transparent cases with just the right amount of jewelry on display. This was very important, her mother told her, to have just the right amount of jewelry on display. If there was too much on display, the store was considered gaudy and cheap. If there was too little, it was likely stuffy and limited. "Jewelry stores want to have just enough to entice you to enter," she said, "while concealing just enough to ensure you stay." This window had just the right amount. Her mother liked the window very much, and she was very excited for them to go inside. Her mother then walked to the heavy glass door and pulled it open so that her daughter could walk through.

As soon as she walked through the doors, she immediately felt the warm light, which was different from the natural light she felt on the street. Inside, the place was aglow, with lights filling the room for the sole purpose of displaying the jewels that filled the glass cases—diamond necklaces, rings, earrings, bracelets, brooches, decorative pins, and elegant watches, crafted in platinum and gold, bejeweled and decadent. It was magnificent, the daughter thought, something of a fantasyland cut from every fairy tale ever conceived. It affected her deeply and spoke to her, the utter beauty of it all, tucked inside, warm and safe while the cars and people rushed by on the busy street outside the window. There was something just so refined and pristine, like being in a museum, only the artists were craftsmen. It was truly stunning, and she never forgot the feeling she had that first moment she entered the store.

After they had spent a few minutes looking interestingly in the glass cases filled with jewelry, a woman approached her mother and inquired politely, "*Señora*, would you like to see a piece of jewelry?" The young girl watched her mother very carefully, the way she had garnered the salesperson's attention, and the manner she responded, which was interested but not overeager.

"Perhaps in a bit," said my mother. "Thank you for offering. I may want to look at a piece or two."

The salesperson appreciated the mother's response. It had been respectful and grateful and showed enough serious interest for the salesperson to remain observant but not pushy.

"What do you think of this place?" the mother whispered softly to the daughter. "Do you like it?"

"I love it, Mother," replied the daughter. "It is beautiful."

"Yes, it is," replied the mother. "It is beautiful. It is a beautiful store, with many beautiful things. Beautiful is a perfect way to describe it. I agree."

The young girl seemed very happy with this response, and they looked around the store, gazing into each case, for quite some time. The mother asked the daughter which pieces of jewelry she liked most, and she pointed to a yellow gold bracelet that was thin and rectangular and shined brightly with small diamonds crafted all around the outside.

"That is a good choice," said the mother. "You have very good taste."

Upon learning this from her daughter, the mother turned to the jeweler and said, "Can you please show me one of the bracelets?"

The jeweler moved swiftly but calmly toward the two of them. She opened the glass case below and reached in to get the bracelet for the mother to see. As she brought the bracelet out from underneath the glass, the girl noticed the jeweler's hands were absolutely flawless, like a porcelain model. She had never seen hands like this before. They looked smooth and soft and without a single mark, almost as if they had gloves around them. The jeweler took the bracelet and laid it across the bones of the mother's wrist in the most delicate, elegant fashion. It was an act so simple and yet it appeared so royal. The mother looked down at her wrist wistfully while her daughter nodded approvingly. It was a very beautiful bracelet, and it looked even better on the mother's hand with her fine clothes and new haircut.

"How do you like it?" asked the woman with the impeccable hands.

"I like it," said the mother. "I like it very much. It is an exceptional bracelet. But I am not sure if I am going to purchase it today or not."

"Either way, you should try it with the matching ring, earrings, and necklace," said the woman at the store. "Here, let me just show you the four pieces all together."

The woman brought out the other pieces of jewelry. Each piece was very expensive and, truth be told, the mother had no intention of purchasing them, much as she would have enjoyed doing so. But she knew how to work the room, and she knew that she had the jeweler's attention. The scene was all very well crafted with her daughter looking on intently.

"I am just not sure," said the mother.

"It's no problem at all," said the woman at the store. "Let me show you."

With that, she assembled the expensive pieces of jewelry in perfect order. She lined them up with her perfect hands and her impeccable manners and she adorned the girl's mother in diamonds and gold. She closed the clasp of the necklace around the mother's neck as if she were royalty, and the mother looked absolutely ready to walk the red carpet draped in the extravagant jewels. She was stunning, absolutely stunning. There was no other word for it. She really was exceptional, and on that day, her daughter saw her mother differently.

The daughter saw her mother as she had never seen her before. She watched her face light up, the years roll away, and a thousand dreams (that she must have had at one time) return in an instant. She saw an elegant debutant, ready for the ball, who would turn every head that passed by, and she was inspired by the transformation of body and spirit that the jewelry could perpetuate. She even saw her giggle, the way a schoolgirl might. The daughter had never seen her mother giggle before, and she had only witnessed a grown woman giggling in the movies, when a leading lady knew she had the upper hand and was holding all the cards.

It was at that moment that the girl knew definitively what she wanted to do when she was older. One day she too would be a jeweler. She would go to work each day surrounded by diamonds and gold and platinum. She would dress proper and professional and she would have perfect, porcelain hands that lifted the jewelry and fastened it with the utmost care. Although she had decided at that very moment that she wanted to be a jeweler, the young girl did not tell her mother at the time. She just looked on, in awe, while her mother shined brighter than she had ever seen in all her years.

When they returned home that night, the mother asked her daughter if she enjoyed their day together. "I enjoyed it very much, Mother," she said. "You looked like a movie star, and I liked seeing you in all of the jewelry."

"I am no movie star," said her mother. "But I am so glad you enjoyed it. I had fun too."

Although the vision of her mother had been incredibly striking, the young girl couldn't stop thinking about the jeweler and, most noticeably, the jeweler's hands. She had never seen hands like that before, and she wondered how they came to be that way. Was she born with perfect hands? How did she care for them? It was clear by the shape of her fingers that she had never broken any bones, but the skin seemed even more remarkable. How was it so impossibly smooth and clean and soft? What did the jeweler do to take care of her hands? They were clearly important to her, and there was no question she went to great lengths to maintain them in such a pristine manner.

All these years later, the experience the girl had with her mother continued to resonate. The impact of that day at the jewelry store was lasting, and she thought about her mother each day when she went to work. She thought about her when she watched a woman walk through the doors of her store and particularly when that young woman was accompanied by her daughter. Was the woman actually a potential customer or was she merely out for a day with her daughter, a day to feel like a queen, to be pampered and doted on?

Although this question crossed the jeweler's mind, she treated each customer the same—by showing them the most exceptional care. They all received the royal treatment. They all deserved the royal treatment, and it was her hope that when they walked out of her store, they felt like they had obtained an experience different from any other they had ever received in a jewelry store. She went to great lengths to make sure she was attentive but never obtrusive. She knew the specific details of every piece—carat, weight, clarity, etc., and she was even well versed in the origin of the materials. There wasn't anything she didn't know about her jewelry, and she prided herself in being an expert regarding every aspect of the items she sold.

When she thought of that day with her mother, she could easily recall just how beautiful her mother looked wearing the jewelry. She had hoped that one day her mother would, in fact, be able to own a piece of jewelry like the ones she tried on in the store. Their family didn't have that kind of money, and she was sure her mother never gave it more than a brief, passing thought. But she had thought of it a great deal. She had thought of the way her mother looked at herself in the mirror, and she wished her mother could feel that way, really feel that way, beyond simply a moment playing a charade in an elegant jewelry store.

It wasn't so much the pieces of jewelry that stood out in her mind as the way they had made her mother feel, the attitude inside her that the jewelry had brought out. It could be seen in the way she stood up straight, arched her back, and peered out from behind her eyes with a coolness she had never witnessed before in her mother. These aspects weren't just a charade, but a part of her mother's being that had been suppressed for all these years. A part that had been subdued in the unflinching face of reality. Quelled in the long shadow of what was possible. But they were there, dormant, deep down on the inside, and it made the jeweler sad to think of the lengths her mother must have had to go to in order to conceal them.

It was a Tuesday morning in early November. The holiday season had yet to arrive, and the city was quiet. The summer and fall tourism had dissipated, and people were back to doing their daily jobs, going about their daily lives, and enjoying the slightly dulled senses that come with those brief periods in our lives that feel impossibly normal. The weather was beginning to turn, and the skies were now gray. It was a moment in time when the entire city just felt exhausted and in need of catching its collective breath. Even those Catalans who so desperately pined for their independence had called a temporary ceasefire. The city was quiet, at least as quiet as Barcelona ever got, and the jeweler didn't have many customers enter the store.

However, she was a perfectionist, a real perfectionist, and she had been this way ever since she had gone to the jewelry store with her mother. Her job, after all, demanded it, and there was no margin for error. There wasn't even a little room to be "less than" or "sufficient," and everything about being a jeweler centered around being prepared, every day, at all times, to offer someone an experience they would never forget. She took this responsibility seriously, and there wasn't anything else that meant more to her.

Since the store was so quiet on this day, she put gloves on her perfect hands and took out the glass cleaner. Although the cases looked immaculate to the naked eye, there was always room for improvement, and she carefully ensured that every partial fingerprint or smudge was removed. Once this task was complete, she moved to the pieces of jewelry in the store and began polishing them, one piece at a time, carefully, while people walked past her door and the sky remained gray outside the large, glass windows of the store. She performed this entire process with her reading glasses sitting atop her nose. Ever since she had turned forty-five, she needed reading glasses. It had become difficult to read words up close. They weren't as clear as they once were, and polishing her jewelry was much like reading a book. Every detail was important, and she couldn't afford to strain her eyes, much less miss something of monumental importance.

Once she finished polishing the jewelry, she reached up with her right hand and removed her glasses from her face. She placed them inside a cloth case and tucked them back into her purse. Then she pulled the gloves off her hands, revealing her long fingers and her porcelain skin, now wet with sweat from having been inside the gloves, working. She wiped her hands gently, locked the store temporarily, and then disappeared into the back to wash her hands thoroughly, put lotion on, and care for them as she always did. This was her routine, particularly when the store was not busy, and she liked to stick to her routine. It made her feel good to stick to her routine, and the store looked spectacular, with the jewelry gleaming inside the glass cases.

The jeweler's store would only be open until lunch today, which was two o'clock in Spain. People ate lunch later in the day in Spain, and the jeweler decided she would not open the store in the evening. Besides, she had plans for lunch.

Just before she was set to close the store, her mother walked in with another woman. She was an old woman now, and she now walked unsteadily but still with more than a hint of dignity.

"This is a beautiful store," remarked her mother, looking around at the glistening jewels.

"You are very kind to say that," remarked the daughter.

"Would you mind if I try on that bracelet?" asked her mother, pointing to one inside a case.

"It hasn't been one of her good days," said the woman, who was her mother's caregiver, with her mother not seeming to notice. "You know how it is."

"Of course," said the jeweler as she reached into the case for the bracelet. "It's fine. I understand."

"Here you go, *Señora*," said the daughter, as she fastened the bracelet around her mother's wrist. "It looks absolutely lovely."

Her mother didn't say anything for a few minutes. She looked at her face in the small mirror on the counter almost in search of herself. She had to be in there somewhere. She then dropped her head and gazed down at the bracelet stretched out elegantly across her wrist. Her mother smiled. Eventually, the caregiver reminded her mother that they were going to lunch with her daughter today and that they could come back to the store another time if she wanted.

The mother then placed her wrist on the counter, while her daughter delicately opened the clasp and removed the bracelet.

"You have such beautiful hands," her mother remarked. "They are smooth and soft and look like porcelain."

Her daughter blushed a little and then offered. "That is very nice of you to say."

"Well ... it is absolutely true," stated her mother. "They are the most beautiful hands I have ever seen."

# LINO

How long had Lino been driving a taxi? He couldn't even remember. But he could remember how long he loved Lisbon. From the first moment, he thought. It must have been then. Perhaps before that, before he even met her. For as long as there was time itself, from the days when it was called Olissipo and Olissipona, it seemed he must have loved her, even before he knew she existed.

His love for Lisbon was different from a love experienced through sight, but rather one steeped in feeling, in the memory of feelings, and in memory itself if that was indeed possible. For Lino, those memories seemed to be woven intricately into the fabric of his DNA, a part of his soul long before they were a part of his psyche. It didn't seem to him that he had to recall his feelings about the city or the obscure facts he knew about her. He couldn't even remember where he had obtained each piece of information, but the knowledge became embedded. It was now his. It had always been his.

Perhaps it was in his DNA. His family had lived in Lisbon for many years, generations in reality. His mother was Spanish, but his father was born in Lisbon. Just as his grandfather had been and his great-grandfather before that and on and on for as many generations as they could trace. Lisbon had been home to his ancestors through the wars and political shifts and fires and earthquakes that tore the city apart. It had been their home through the night and the day, the light and the dark, the Moors and the Christians. Through it all, Lisbon remained resolute, proud, and above all … theirs.

If there is a constant theme in Lisbon's history, it is rebirth. The city has been forced to rebuild time and time again. The circumstances have varied, but the reality has been the same. The catastrophic loss of beauty and the responsibility to reclaim it. The duty to rebuild and to be reborn. It was as if the soul of Lisbon was continually being tested. The buildings may have changed, but the heartbeat of the city was eternal, immovable, and unflinching. The will of the people couldn't be eliminated, and each new

Lisbon was new only on the exterior. The core was made from the same fabric, the type of material that couldn't be burned in a fire or shaken by a seismic shift. Lino loved this about Lisbon above all else.

Lino liked driving a taxi. He liked it very much, and he was happy to spend his days transporting people around Lisbon. He had not settled for this profession. He had arrived at it, perhaps even been drawn toward it, surprisingly—the happiest type of accident imaginable. We don't always begin where we end or end where we begin, he thought. You never know where the winds will blow, but life, like Lisbon, requires the ability to be reborn.

From the first day he started driving, he felt happier. Lino hadn't liked his old job but, behind the wheel, he could experience the Lisbon he loved most. Moving with people. Alive. This was how he felt. Like Lisbon, Lino had been reborn, with the eternal spirit of the city flowing in his blood day and night, as he drove down the alleyways and up the great hills, shuttling people to and from their destinations.

Lino's job paid well enough, and he had some flexibility with his hours. Beyond the practical aspects, he was good at it. His father had taught him how to drive a manual transmission long before he would have been legally allowed to drive, and he was a very patient teacher. "That's OK Lino," he would say when the car stalled out. Lino would sigh and lose confidence until his father placed his arm on his shoulder and said "That happens to everyone. Try again. You'll get it."

Although he likely went through a clutch or two, Lino did get it. He got it like few people ever have. One day, it just clicked. Suddenly he was able to transform what his father was communicating into practice. It felt completely natural, as if he had been doing it for years. There wasn't a single hitch from that day on, and it was not dissimilar to his knowledge of Lisbon in that it had effectively become a part of him, regardless of its origins. His father didn't act surprised at all. He was a man who was rarely surprised, and he didn't act. He merely said, "There you go, Lino. Very nice. I told you that you would get it."

Lino never forgot the unwavering confidence his father had shown. It was blind faith. After all, Lino had done nothing to give his father an inkling that he would ever be a good driver. He had given him only doubt, and yet his father had shown faith. This was a lesson Lino would never forget, and he often thought about how close he had been to giving up on driving, how easy it would have been for him to quit this thing he now performed so exquisitely were it not for his father.

Behind the wheel, he could feel the pedals like they were an extension of his legs, his feet, his will, his soul. Whenever the situation called for it, he could play with the pedals effortlessly, calculating precisely the right amount of throttle to offer even the steepest inclines. Whether he was easing around the shoreline, past the Tower of Belem or climbing the mystic streets in the Alfama district toward Castelo Sao Jorge, the car responded to his every whim. It almost seemed to urge to please him, and when there was a moment when the engine might have feigned the difficulty of climbing higher, he heard his father's voice and he would speak to the taxi itself and say calmly, "It's OK. You'll get it."

When he sped by the port, he recalled those mornings when his father took him down to the docks to meet the men who hauled cargo on and off ships. His father, who worked for the postal service, revered the men who worked on ships, whose bodies were blessed with a sturdiness his did not possess. The men were always glad to see Lino. They were glad to see his father too, and they liked the way his father introduced Lino to them. He treated these hulking men of the sea as if they were great dignitaries of the world, superheroes of vital importance, and they felt his respect. Lino gazed up at them with awe, watched them strain their backs as they hoisted containers and boxes, sweat pouring over their dirt-stained faces. It was impressive, and the men worked even harder when Lino and his father watched them as the sun came up over the city and the birds flew back and forth along the shore.

In many ways, these men were as important as his father made them seem. Shipping and trade had been a part of Lisbon's history for as long as the city had stood, perched along the western edge of the European continent. From the port in Lisbon, both the Atlantic and the Mediterranean were equally accessible, and ships could sail for the Middle East, Africa, and the Americas from here. Vasco da Gama's fleet had sailed to India from Lisbon and Amerigo Vespucci had sailed from Lisbon as well. It was a place where great men had come and gone, as far back as Ulysses, who many believe had landed here with his men on the way home from Troy. Lisbon had been an important city. It was an important city. The sea helped make it important, and it had been that way for centuries. The men who worked on the docks were part of that history, a distinguished part, and Lino's father made sure Lino understood that.

As Lino drove through the storied streets of Lisbon, he thought about his father. Lino never knew his mother. She had died during his birth, and he had only a picture. She was beautiful, with long black hair and the type of mystery in her eyes that was needed to convince a Spanish woman to move to Portugal. His father said her beauty was the only beauty that compared to Lisbon. When she died, his father knew he would not remarry. He would do his best to raise Lino. He could never be a mother, and he knew Lino would never know a mother's touch. The closest thing Lino would ever know to a mother would be Lisbon. He had only Lisbon.

Lino was only twenty-nine when his father died. The diagnosis had caught him off guard. There was no fair warning. No time to prepare. No. When his father became ill, only a single trip to the doctor was needed to deliver the bad news. It was cancer. It had spread. They would try to prolong his life for as long as possible, but that was all they could do. Lino and his father sat there listening quietly. His father never took his eyes off the doctor. He never lowered his head, and he didn't cry. He looked straight ahead until the doctor was finished. Then he turned to Lino and said, "It will be OK."

As the cancer spread into his bones, Lino's father was unable to walk distances. He liked to walk, and he was sad not to be able to stroll in the morning light with the smell of the sea wafting through the painted streets. And so he called Lino to give him a ride in his taxi every day. He wasn't looking for special favors. He was looking for transportation—to the doctor, to lunch with friends, back to his small apartment. At first, Lino thought he was joking, but his father didn't joke much. "I am calling for a taxi," he said. "Is this the right number?"

When Lino arrived in his taxi, he would hustle around the vehicle to open the door for his father. His father had taught him that it was proper to open doors for people, and Lino always did this. Despite Lino's best efforts, his father refused to sit in the front seat. "The front seat is only for when the meter is off," he would say. "I am a customer, and I prefer to sit in the back." Lino informed him that his money was no good here. He had done more for his son than Lino could ever repay, and Lino couldn't bear to collect his father's money. But his father corrected him. "It is impossible to repay someone for their love, indecent even," said his father. "My love is given without thought of a single reciprocity. This is your work, and I insist on paying the fare. After all, I am riding with the finest taxi driver in Lisbon."

His father always seemed to know how to say the right thing. He always had. He said the right thing and he did the right thing. The clothes don't make the man, but Lino's father also dressed impeccably. "My clothes are not to impress others," he would say "but rather out of respect for them." Some of this was generational, but Lino's father took particular pride in his appearance. Even as his hair evaporated and his waist shrunk, he would venture out into the world—shirt pressed, shoes shined, a fine coat, and always with a dignified hat. There were no apparent riches to behold, but a measure of class that was unmistakable. You could buy a nice suit, but class couldn't be purchased. It was either in you or nowhere to be found. Lino's father had it in spades.

Lino very much enjoyed serving as his father's driver during these final days. He knew all the streets from years of exploring the city with his dad and even found some new routes from his time behind the wheel. "That's interesting," his father would say when he found a shortcut. "Very nice, Lino," his father would exclaim when his son threaded the needle of a crooked street to evade a series of lights and traffic. His driving style was smooth. It was smooth and there was no evidence of those first days when he struggled to get a feel for the clutch. Lino was now an artist. He had become a masterful driver, and his father was impressed with the manner in which Lino navigated the myriad of tight corners and cobblestone streets so effortlessly. It was a thing of beauty, he thought. Truly beautiful, unrivaled, and it reminded him only of the beauty of his wife and of Lisbon.

As he drove his father around town, the city provided an exquisite canvas for Lino to paint an oratory masterpiece of their life together. Along the coastline, he recalled those days in the early morning with the great men at the docks. When they climbed in the Alfama district, Lino recalled the first time his father took him to the cathedral and how they ate pastries afterward from the mirador. Or the time he had fallen off his bike on a hill and gashed his knee. He recalled the gentle way his father picked him up in the street and carried him to the sidewalk. "It's OK, Lino," he heard his father say. "You're OK. It will be OK." His father simply sat quietly in the back seat, listening to the stories roll off Lino's tongue. He fashioned a subtle glimpse of a smile across his withering lips. "I remember," he said. "I remember it all very well."

His father lived as long as he was able. As the cancer spread, the pain grew. But he never complained. He just eased into the back of the taxi each day and said "It's alright, Lino. It will be OK." And then one day he was gone.

A number of years passed. Lino drove effortlessly through the city. He now had a family of his own—two girls and a boy. He had fallen in love, with an American who was studying at the university in Lisbon. She was enchanted by the city's colors and taken by Lino's connection to every shade of Lisbon. He swept her off her feet, and they were happy in Lisbon.

By this time, just about everyone in Lisbon knew Lino. He had made a real name for himself. If you were in need of transport, he was simply the man to call. There was no finer driver, and whether you wanted to see the sights, go to the airport, or visit the *mercado*, he was your man. Some people even ignored every expense to hire Lino to take them on a day trip to Sintra. He was that good.

It was a morning like any other. Lisbon was gleaming in the early sun. The Tagus River looked majestic, as it swept under a series of bridges. The Belem Tower was illuminated perfectly against the backdrop of blue sky.

Lino pulled over at Praca do Comercio, near the Arco da Rua Augusta, to pick up what appeared to be a woman and her daughter. Lino leaped out of the car and hustled to open the door as he always did. This caught the women by surprise, but they thanked Lino for the gesture and slid carefully into the backseat. The young woman was in her early twenties and carrying a backpack. Her mother was in her mid-fifties, with a purse slung over her right shoulder and her left hand carrying a small leather case just below her waist. Lino offered for the ladies to place their bags in the trunk in order to provide them with more room in the back seat, but they preferred to keep their bags with them.

The mother asked Lino to drive them to the Castelo Sao Jorge atop a great hill in the Alfama district. He had been there many times with his father, and the castle offered some of the best views of the city.

When Lino looked in the rearview mirror, he saw the mother pull her daughter close, and the daughter's head now rested on the mother's chest. "It's OK," she said to her daughter. "Everything will be OK."

As the car headed upward, the daughter said to her mother, "I'm not ready."

"I know," said the mother. "I am not sure anyone ever is."

"Do we have to do this today?" asked the daughter.

"Honey, it's time," said the mother. "We are here in Lisbon. The day is just beginning, and the city is ready too."

"But I am not," said the daughter.

"I understand," said the mother.

Lino turned down a quiet street and pointed the car uphill toward the Church of Saint Anthony.

"But why do we have to let him go? I don't understand. Shouldn't he stay with us?"

"I wish he could," said the mother

"He still can," the daughter replied.

"We've had him for a long time," said the mother. "It wasn't nearly enough, but nobody belongs to anyone forever."

"I don't think that's true," said the daughter. "Can't he stay just a little longer?"

"No, he can't," said the mother. "It was his wish to be set free. This is what he wanted. We must respect that."

"It's just so hard," said the daughter, now whimpering against her mother's gray, silk shirt.

The mother curled her right arm around her daughter's shoulder, with her left arm resting lovingly around the leather case that sat next to her on the back seat.

"I know it is, sweetheart. It's not easy for me either. But your father specifically stated that he wanted his ashes spread in Lisbon. This was the place where he proposed to me, and Lisbon was the first place we took you as a child. You know how he adored Lisbon."

"Yes, but we live in London. Our home is in London. He lived in London," said the daughter.

Lino sat quietly behind the wheel and said nothing. There was nothing to say, really, but he still couldn't avoid wiping the tears that were now leaking down his face as he worked the pedals on the steep incline. He had tried to conceal his emotions, but it was to no avail. Lino was a sensitive man, but he felt guilty that he had now intruded on such a private moment. He apologized and offered his condolences to the mother and daughter for their loss.

When they got as close to the castle as they could, Lino pulled the car over to the side of the road. "My father took me here for my tenth birthday," he said. "We didn't have money for a party, and so he took me here … bought me gelato in that store right there with the turquoise sign, before we walked up to the castle and out to the mirador and looked over the city. This great city. This magical city of dreams and ships and churches and hills and explorers, this city of different races, religions, creeds, and colors. My dad guided my eyes from the Tagus River to Praca do Comercia where I picked you up to the Alfama district to Rossi Square, the Santa Justa Elevator, and all the way up to Eduardo VII Park. It was in the late afternoon, and I can recall the colors being summoned to life with each moment as the sun began its dramatic descent. My father has been gone for more than ten years, but I always think of him when I come here. It is a beautiful place."

The mother and daughter sat quietly listening, and Lino wondered if he had overstepped his boundaries sharing the memory of his birthday here with his own father. The two women remained in the back seat, heads slightly bowed, and neither moved for the door. Finally, the daughter spoke. "Thank you for sharing that story. It was very kind of you. I am glad this is a special place."

"Yes, thank you," said the mother, and they began to move for the doors.

Lino was somewhat out of his depth now. Behind the wheel, he always knew what to do. It was instinctive and natural, and he never had to think about how much gas to give the throttle. But this was different. Even so, he couldn't help himself. He had heard the conversation between the mother and daughter. He knew they were in pain. Though he was in no position to offer them advice or comfort, he went ahead and spoke. "I … I am sorry," he said prefacing his intrusion, "but would you mind if I show you one more part of the city?"

The mother looked at the daughter. The daughter's eyes pleaded with her to accept Lino's invitation. Anything that might prolong the inevitable task they were charged with felt like a gift to the daughter. The mother hesitated and then said reluctantly, "I suppose that would be alright."

"Thank you," said Lino.

Lino drove down from the castle, past the Lisbon Cathedral, the oldest building in the city, and headed for the docks. There were freighters in the port along with a cruise ship, and the marina was filled with boats. He got out and raced around to open the door for the two ladies. They grabbed their bags and stepped out of the car.

"Follow me," said Lino.

They followed Lino to one of the docks in the marina where two older men were getting ready to take their fishing boat out for the day when they saw Lino approach them. They set down the nets, smiled, took off their caps in respect, and stepped off the boat and onto the dock.

"Well, if it isn't Paulo's boy", said Gustavo, the bigger of the two men.

"Hasn't changed a bit," said João, the smaller man. "All those mornings at the docks with his dad. You would have thought he was going to be a fisherman."

Gustavo and João had been working the docks for as long as Lino could remember. In their younger years, when their tense muscles rippled across their backs and their strong arms protruded magnificently through their shirts, these men worked in the day and night hoisting cargo on and off ships. Now they were old men. They were old men who could no longer lift the heavy cargo. But they still came to the port every day, and they now worked the fishing boats that trawled the local waters. Each morning, they lolled their aging frames from their beds and set out to do a job, just as they had the day before and the day before that. All these years later, they remained real heroes to Lino and he held them in the same high regard he felt when his father first introduced them to Lino all those years ago.

Just as they did when his father had come around in the old days, they seemed to work a little harder when Lino came by, and they quickened the pace, untangling the nets on the dock in preparation for the day's work. Lino introduced them to the two women and then asked them if he could chat with them for a moment privately. "Wait here," he said to the young woman and her mother.

Lino asked Gustavo and João if they could take the two women out on the boat that morning, with the sun still rising, the bridges aglow with light and the smell of the sea just taking hold in the shadow of Lisbon perched on the hill. He would come on the boat with them, of course, and he promised to cover all their costs as well as whatever they forfeited in wages for the day. Lino came down to the docks to visit the men from time to time, but he had never asked anything of them. He had never made a single request, and they knew this was important to him.

"Happy to do it, Lino," said Gustavo.

"For Paulo's boy," said João, hoisting a beer in the early morning to Lino's dad. "To Paulo," he said. "A prince among men in fair Lisbon."

The boat pushed off smoothly into the harbor. The water was quiet and calm and the men liked it this way. The city had yet to wake up, and the earth emanated with a peaceful serenity it only offered at this time of day, the time of day when great men hoisted cargo in the early morning, when the rigs were prepared, and when Lino's dad used to take his boy down to the port to see the Lisbon of the great seas come to life.

The mother and daughter looked back at the beautiful city he loved so much. It looked even more beautiful from the water and more beautiful than it had ever looked before. The mother could understand why her husband loved it so, and her daughter could see why it was a special place.

"Vasco da Gama set out from here in 1497 with four ships and 170 men," said Gustavo. "Sailed around the tip of Africa and made it to India."

Lino stood by himself on the deck. He watched the mother and daughter sitting side by side, the mother still holding the leather case. He thought of his father. He liked to think of his father. It made him feel good to think of those mornings at the port watching the men. His father quiet and alert, watching the men work, and admiring this great city and all it took to make it go day after day, all the efforts to rebuild it time and time again in order to match the wondrous beauty it had attained. Lino walked to the front of the boat to thank Gustavo and João. He thanked them as the three men stood there admiring the city they loved so much.

When the men turned, they noticed that the mother and daughter had stood up. Their backs were turned, and they had opened the case. Inside it was a yellow vase. The yellow vase contained the ashes of the man who had been both husband and father, who had loved the two of them and loved Lisbon. Without saying anything they grabbed the gilded vase from inside the case and, holding it together, raised it above their shoulders and set him free over the Tagus River. The mother and daughter and Lino and the men on the boat watched him swirling elegantly against the beautiful blue backdrop, in a touch of wind that seemed to have been summoned in the clear, morning air with the gulls overhead, the bridges lining the distance and the pastel colors of Lisbon watching over them from the shore. There were no words needed and none worthy of the moment.

The men on the boat were old. They had been on many voyages. And it would have seemed as if they were much closer to the end than the beginning. Perhaps that was not the case. Perhaps the beautiful burial they had witnessed wasn't the end of something, but rather the beginning. A new beginning. The commencement of a long and beautiful journey in a different form.

They weren't sure they believed that, but it made them feel good to pretend. They felt good with the sun hitting their faces on the water and so much of their life already behind them.

"You can travel to just about anywhere in the world from this spot," said Gustavo. "Just about anywhere," he said breaking the long silence following the burial at sea.

"Very true," said João. "Just as easy to reach the coast of Africa as the sun topped beaches of Bermuda or the

Virgin Islands. "You can even drift to Manhattan from here or head north to Ireland, the land of Yeats, eternal at Innisfree."

"Of course, the Mediterranean is always glorious—from the Amalfi Coast to the Greek Islands where the gods once bathed," added Gustavo.

Lisbon and the mouth of the Tagus was, after all, a gateway to the world, linking the East and West and cities great and small. This was the place where explorers set sail, where great men hoisted cargo onto ships, and all those who left were destined to return, to rise from the ashes, to live eternal and be reborn time and time again.

For a long time, they all just sat there quietly. Gustavo had cut the motor, and they could hear the water against the side of the boat. Eventually, Gustavo and João guided the boat back to the shore. Lino thanked them graciously, and the mother held her daughter's hand. They said goodbye to the men on the boat. Lino walked the mother and daughter to his car and drove them back up the hill, navigating the cobblestone corridors effortlessly, past the Lisbon Cathedral to the Castelo Sao Jorge. It was nearly midday. The sun was warm, and the tourists were beginning to arrive. Lino opened the back door and said goodbye to the two women. They thanked him underneath the great, swooping trees that sat at the foot of the castle. He was an exceptional taxi driver, they thought, the most exceptional they had ever seen.

The sun was now high in the sky. Afternoon was moving in with certainty. Lino sat back down in the driver's seat, placed his hands on the leather steering wheel and easily shifted the car into gear. In the rearview mirror, he saw the mother wrap her arm around the daughter's shoulder, as they walked slowly toward the *gelateria* with the turquoise sign, in the city he loved so much.

# ABOUT THE AUTHOR

David Joseph's writing has been published in *The Wall Street Journal*, *LA Times*, *London Magazine*, *DoubleTake Magazine*, *Motherwell*, *The Plain Dealer*, and *Rattle*. His first book, a collection of poems entitled *The White Pigeon*, was published in 2002 by Galt Art House. He is a graduate of Hobart College and the University of Southern California's Graduate Writing Program, where he was a recipient of the Kerr Fellowship and served as editor for the *Southern California Anthology*. In 2002, he Co-Founded the Nonprofit organization America SCORES LA, and he received The John Henry Hobart Fellowship for Ethics and Social Justice in 2007. He has taught at Pepperdine University and Harvard University. In 2019, he was awarded a position on the Fulbright Specialist Roster.

Made in the USA
Coppell, TX
29 May 2021

56554249R00139